M000169809

SUSPECT
BEHAVIOR

by

Quashon Davis

Suspect Behavior

Copyright © 2018 by Quashon Davis

Gramma,

This one is for you.

You loved a good book.

I miss you and will continue to make you proud.

New York City.

IT'S ABOUT 10:00 AM, but all the noise and people the city puts out are being muffled inside the thick walls of the Hotel Meridian. It's one of the oldest buildings in the city. The giant pillars and high ceilings not only keep the elegance, they help the structure survive the test of time. Inside the executive suite on the top floor, sits a chubby Italian man. He has spent several minutes looking at a baby picture he keeps in a small locket around his neck. Nervous and lightly sweating, the picture of his son is somewhat calming to him. One of his henchmen walks up to him and lets him know it's time to go. The doors to room 111 open and six large men step out, wearing black suits and shades. They look around and signal back into the room. Out steps the short, Italian man, with a nervous look on his face. Behind him, four more large men bring up the rear. They head for the elevator quickly and quietly. As they all squeeze into the tiny space, the guards are careful to keep the small man in the middle. When they get to the ground floor, the men in front look around quickly as they all get out. There are a few people in the lobby, but no one really pays them any attention. As they make their way past the front desk, there's a Hindu woman holding her crying baby. Her face and body are covered with a bright gold veil and dupatta. Her baby drops his bottle on the floor as the entourage walks by. They all ignore her and begin to step over it. Vito Citronelli, the old mob boss, picks it up and hands it back to the woman.

"Thank you, kind sir." She bows.

The men get outside and pile into two large black sedans. They quickly pull off and speed down the street.

"See? You got nothing to worry about, boss. No one can get to you. We'll be at the courthouse in five minutes," says one of the men.

"I've got plenty to worry about. I didn't think I would make it to even see this day. Testifying against the other mob bosses? Clearly, I must be nuts," proclaims the short, Italian man.

"Boss, come on, you got a sweet deal. You made millions and the government knows it. All you gotta do is point fingers at the other crime families and you aint gotta go to jail. They're gonna set you up somewhere else with a new identity. You got it made," says Florentino, his best henchman.

"Sure doesn't feel like I got it made," he says, looking nervously out the window.

"Relax, boss. They'll all be in jail anyway." The driver says, quickly looking back.

"Yeah, but I've become the one thing I despise, a rat. We don't tell on each other in this business, kid. It's an unwritten rule. The only good rat is a dead rat. I've had men killed for squealing. Now, in a couple of hours, I'll be the squealer."

"You had no choice, boss," says Florentino.

"There's always a choice, kid. I woulda did the time, but I need to be around for my kid. My father wasn't around to tell me right from wrong, and I ended up in this life. I can't put him through that."

"I understand," Florentino says, while removing his shades.

As they pull up to the courthouse, there are reporters and cameras everywhere. They rush up to the two cars, trying to get pictures and interviews before the doors even open.

"You ready to go out there, boss?" the driver asks.

There's no answer. The short chubby man coughs a couple of times. He then continuously coughs. The coughing begins to get uncomfortable.

"Boss? You okay?"

The coughing becomes violent. He doubles over and begins frothing at the mouth. The coughing has now turned into a seizure. His guards are in a panic.

"Get us to the hospital," one of them yells.

It's already too late. The "Boss" leans all the way over and lightly tumbles to the floor of the car.

"H-He's dead," one of the men says.

"What the hell happened?"

"I don't know."

"What the hell do you mean?"

"He was fine a minute ago," Florentino says nervously.

The reporters and cameramen are up against the car windows, snapping pictures and frantically trying to get into position.

"Get us outta here now," one of the men says to the driver.

The two sedans speed away from the courthouse.

CHAPTER ONE
THE RETURN

INSIDE PRECINCT 73, CAPTAIN DON Rayton is losing his mind. The veteran police chief has been dealing with calls, press, and every other stressor possible since the news broke about the mysterious death of Vito Citronelli, the mob boss who was set to testify against five other mob factions. What was going to be the highest profile case the city has seen in years just became even higher. Captain Rayton and his signature, long gray moustache is at the end of their rope.

"Dammit, somebody better tell me something. This guy was put up in a hotel where nobody, except his own people had access to him. What the hell happened?"

"The autopsy is gonna take a while, Captain. We just don't know," says Officer Pete Stapleton, who's definitely not one of his favorites.

"Didn't I just ask for some goddamn answers?"

"Yes, sir."

"Do you have some goddamn answers?"

"No, sir."

"Then shut the hell up and find me some. A material witness in the biggest trial we've had in years doesn't just die for no reason. Somebody killed him. Maybe the other crime bosses flipped one of Citronelli's people. Somebody somewhere knows what happened. I damn well better know by the end of the day."

"Captain, the *New York Post* is on line three," a woman says, walking up to him.

"Tell them I don't know shit. When I know shit, I'll fling it in their direction."

"Yes, sir."

"Captain, I may have something," a young officer says.

"What?"

"Witnesses said that they saw what appeared to be a Hindu woman in the lobby. One even said that at one point, either she or her baby dropped a bottle on the floor, and Citronelli picked it up and gave it back to her."

"So?"

"His symptoms were consistent with poison, sir."

The captain stops and takes a long tug on his old, gray beard.

"Tell the coroner to check for every type of poison known to man. Get on the phone with that hotel and find out the names of every guest last night. Get them to send over the surveillance tapes."

"Right away, Captain."

As Rayton turns to head back to his desk, two men in dark suits walk up. They ignore everyone and everything around them, focusing on the captain. He immediately rolls his eyes when he spots them.

"Are you Captain Don Rayton?" one of them asks.

"Yeah. What do you want? I'm kinda busy."

"Is there somewhere we can talk?" one of them asks.

"Who the hell are you two supposed to be? *Men in Black*?"

Quashon Davis

"We're FBI, Captain. I'm Agent Austin, and that's Agent Mills."

"Of course. As if my day isn't long enough. Step into my office."

"Captain, there was a major assassination today," says Agent Mills.

"I know that. I have my best people on it."

"I don't think you understand. We think The Ghost assassinated Vito Citronelli," Agent Austin says.

"The Ghost?"

"Yes," Agent Austin continues. "The Ghost is considered to be the best hitman that ever lived. Gets in and out of places with no one ever seeing his face. Thirty confirmed hits. Charges eight million per job. As good as The Ghost is, he was almost caught once. Six years ago, a detective from this precinct almost got him. It's the closest anyone has ever come. We need you to put that detective on this immediately."

"Okay, who was it?"

The two agents look at each other for a second, before Agent Mills responds, "Roger Merrit."

"Ha, ha-ha, ha-ha. Well, I can't help you there. Unless you've been hiding under a rock, you know that Merrit shot one of my officers and fled the country four years ago. He's been in hiding ever since."

"Captain, we think The Ghost is here to assassinate a list of people, important people. We were sent here by the president. He wants Merrit on this," Agent Austin says.

"Did you hear what I said? He shot one of my officers. He fled the country. On top of that, I never liked his ass. He thought he was better than every officer here."

"He was," blurts Agent Mills.

"What?"

3

Mills continues, "Roger Merrit is one of the best detectives that ever lived. His arrest record was incredible. And if we're going to be honest, sir, we're the FBI. We know that he shot Officer Stapleton because he thought he was having an affair with his wife. We know he shot him directly in his vest, just to scare him. We also know his wife was, in fact, seeing one of your officers and they're still together."

"So, what's your point? He's still a fugitive and I don't know where he is."

"He's not a fugitive anymore," Agent Austin says, placing a folder on the captain's desk.

"What the hell is that?"

"That's a full pardon, signed by the president himself. Merrit is fully reinstated." he responds.

"This is the worst day of my life," Rayton says.

"Merrit will be here in twenty-four hours. Make sure he gets whatever he needs," Agent Mills demands.

"You knew where he was the whole damn time?" asks Rayton.

"Of course, we did. We're the FBI. His friend, Jay Jones, sent him to Brazil. We've been monitoring their phone calls for a year and a half," Agent Austin admits.

"You sons of bitches. What about Officer Stapleton? Merrit shot him. He's just supposed to be able to stroll back in here and it's okay? Well, it's not okay. I'm not on board with this B.S. You're creating an uncomfortable environment here. Those officers out there all know what happened. A piece of paper isn't gonna undo all the shit he did."

"We all have our orders, Captain. Although, Officer Stapleton wasn't going to press charges anyway," Agent Mills says.

"I don't like this."

Quashon Davis

"Sounds like you just don't like Merrit, sir. We get it. We read all the files. You had been trying to get rid of him for a while. We're sorry, but The Ghost takes precedence. Citronelli is just the beginning. If our small leads pan out, this city could lose its mayor, and a few other high-profile people. I'm afraid you're going to have to deal with Merrit again. Give him everything he needs," demands Agent Austin.

The agents walk out of Rayton's office. He's so mad he can barely speak.

"I don't believe this. I don't believe this. It can't be happening. God hates me. That's what it is. He hates me. Stapleton, get in here."

"Yes, Captain?"

"The FBI just came in here and told me they're reinstating the man that shot you. They're making Roger Merrit a detective again, here in the same precinct."

"That's cool. He wasn't trying to kill me. I understand why he did it."

"Get the hell out my office, Pete. Now."

"Yes, sir."

"And, send Marie in here."

Captain Rayton paces frantically, trying to figure out what he can do. The anger is giving him vertigo. He's always had a deep hatred for Roger Merrit. He was the best detective Rayton had ever seen, and Merrit knew it. His superior skill set and confidence rubbed Rayton and some of the other older guys the wrong way. They clashed all the time.

"You wanted to see me, Captain?" Marie says.

"You're not gonna believe this, but Roger just got a full pardon and his damn job back."

"What?"

"Yeah. Apparently, the president wants him to go after some hitman. It looks like he was hiding out in Brazil this

5

whole time. I'm guessing you knew that, since you were his partner."

"I did."

"Well, he'll be here in twenty-four hours. You know what I'm gonna do? I'm gonna make you partner up with him again."

"That's not a good idea, Captain."

"Why not, Detective?"

"You know I was seeing his wife. I'm sure he figured that out. We're still together."

"Good. I can't stand him and I want him annoyed and uncomfortable. Him having to partner up with the woman that took his wife from him should piss him off, and throw him off his game."

"With all due respect, Captain, I don't think that's—"

"I'm sorry, Detective, I don't believe I asked you to think. In fact, I didn't ask for your opinion at all. I make the decisions around here. I want the guy uncomfortable. I'm sure he despises you, so you'll be partnering with him again when he gets here. You're dismissed."

Marie walks out of the Captain's office, annoyed, slapping papers to the floor in the hallway. Rayton takes a seat behind his desk, and begins looking over the folder the FBI left behind.

They really knew where this bastard was the whole time, he thinks.

***

Meanwhile, at the theater in Madison Square Garden, retired NBA champion, Jay Jones, is walking through the tunnel. He's preparing to give a speech to the top 100 ranked high school seniors, set to become the next stars of college basketball in the fall. It's been almost four years since Jay played pro ball, but he's still idolized by all of the young guys in the league. All

Quashon Davis

of the high schoolers look up to him, as he was the man on and off the court. When Jay walks in the room, they all go crazy and mob him. From the quietist kid, to the coolest thug; they all melt at the site of the three-time MVP. Jay plays it down, but he loves the attention he gets from the young ballers. He smiles and poses for pictures and selfies with all of them. Their excitement level is more like kids at a carnival, rather than poised high school seniors. In the middle of all the excitement his cell phone begins to ring. He quickly glances at it, planning to put it back in his pocket, but he sees that it's Roger.

"Gimme a quick second, guys. Hey, Raj, what's goin' on? Why are you calling me on my regular number?" he says.

"I'm on my way back," Roger laughs.

"What are you talking about?"

"I got pardoned. All the charges were dropped. I even got my old job back."

"Huh? Are you sure this isn't a trap to lure you back into the country?"

"They sent me the paperwork. I had Danny and two other attorneys look it over. They said it's bulletproof."

"Raj, you're not telling me everything. Why would they just drop the charges against you? Why would they reinstate you? You're a fugitive. How'd they even find you?"

"They found me through you, actually. They knew you were the only friend I had that could fund me leaving the country and surviving. They've been monitoring our calls for a long time, bro."

"Sons of bitches. I don't like that, man. Okay, whatever. Tell me why this is happening and why now?"

"The quick version, a crime boss was about to testify against some other major crime families. He was assassinated. They think it was her."

"The Ghost?"

"Yup."

"You can't go through that again, man. Did you ever even tell them that you figured out it was a woman?"

"Nope."

"You were chasing that woman for two years, Raj. You were losing your mind. You ended up needing counseling. Why put yourself through that again? And, if you ask me, you were falling for her."

"What are you talking about, Jay?"

"The challenge. She kept outsmarting you and it was turning you on. I know you!"

"Listen, I'm exonerated. I even got my old job back. I got no choice. I'm gonna catch her this time."

"What about Miesha, Raj?"

"What about her?"

"She's still legally your wife. She was cheating on you with your old partner. Your old partner, that still works at that same precinct by the way. The guy you shot still works there too. You're just gonna stroll in the front door and it's gonna be all good?"

"I'm over that, Jay. That chapter of my life has been over for years."

"Miesha was the only woman you ever slept with. You married your first and only love. She cheated on you with your partner, your *female* partner. They could still be together for all you know."

"So what? Do you know how many women I've slept with in Brazil these last couple of years?"

"I know you, Raj. I'm gonna say one."

"I hate you."

"I'm right, ain't I?"

"That's a lucky guess, Jay."

8

Quashon Davis

"All I'm saying is there's a lot of emotions that you're not thinking about. I worry about you, man."

"I appreciate that, I really do. I'll be careful. I'm gonna go in there, do my job, and request a transfer out."

"And, you're not gonna kill your old partner, right?"

"Marie? Why would I do that?"

"You know why. She was sneaking around with your wife. I don't trust you, man."

"I'm good, Jay, I promise. I do need a favor though."

"Anything, bro."

Club R & B's Midtown. One of the liveliest spots in the city, they have the motto of always having live music, no matter what. If they're open, there's either a person or a band performing. Thursday is 'Men Lead The Way' night at R & B's, there's a long list of amateur male singers awaiting a chance to show what they can do. The food is also world-renowned, as people not only come for the music. It's a good time all around."

***

For the four women that are out together, this is their favorite night of the month. They get together every first Thursday and come have dinner, listen to the artists and have a good time. They are the epitome of "opposites attract." Maya is a quiet, non-emotional dentist. A former Army sergeant, she doesn't laugh at jokes, doesn't smile at children, and men can't deal with her lack of emotion. Although she claims to be a dentist, no one knows where her office is located. Tall and lean, Maya likes running marathons, and saying no to men.

Angie is the complete opposite of Maya. She's the loudest one of the group, always talking loud and arguing with any and every one. A former senior officer in the Navy, she constantly travels for work, and seems to be a master of put-downs and insults. Angry all the time, Angie is aggressive and feisty when it comes to everything.

Cian is the serious one. She's a security advisor, and travels the world running seminars for defense companies. The former Marine is always focused, always on point, but loves a good time. Cian is a workaholic, always traveling for work, but looks forward to the first Thursday of every month, when she gets together with her friends. She literally plans her work schedule around it.

Tess is a different animal altogether. Once an Army corporal, she travels for leisure twice a month. Her and Maya met as young privates in the Army, and hit it off right away. She claims to have her own business, but no one knows what it is. She has a big house and a nice car, and she's never been married. Her money and attitude intimidates some men, and she likes it. Tess is fine, and financially comfortable.

"You know, I didn't think I was gonna make it tonight," Cian says.

"You say that every month, girl. Get the waiter's attention," laughs Angie.

"You're the one that chooses to work like that. Doesn't make sense to me," says Tess.

"I like to work hard. It makes me feel like I have a purpose."

"I've seen your savings account. You don't need that purpose," says Tess.

The waiter comes over and drops off their bill. He's surprised at how much alcohol they consumed, but happy, thinking about his tip.

"I was at the gym the other day, running on the treadmill, and this tall guy walked by. I've been eyeing him for about two weeks now. He had just finished playing ball and everything. Sweat was everywhere. He stopped right at my treadmill," says Angie.

"So, what happened?" they all ask.

"I got caught up and slid right off the treadmill and fell on the floor."

They all explode with laughter, except for Maya. She just sits there with the same blank expression on her face that she always has.

"That's funny," she says with her blank expression.

The women all stare at her with disapproving faces.

"You're so weird," Cian says.

"For real," Angie agrees.

"I'm not weird."

Just as Maya finishes defending herself, the waiter puts another drink in front of her.

"From the gentlemen at the bar," he says, walking away.

They all turn to see an attractive black man in a suit at the bar, holding up a drink. They all smile and wave except Maya, who holds up the drink and nods at him with her same blank expression.

"What's wrong with you? That man is fine." Angie says.

"He looks young. Young guys drive small cars. I'm tall, so I wouldn't fit."

"Are you really this crazy?"

Before she can answer, the man comes over to their table.

"Good evening, ladies," he says with a smile.

"Good evening," they all say.

"I couldn't help but notice you from where I was sitting. May I ask you your name?"

"I'm Maya."

"Nice name. I'm Trevor."

"Nice to meet you, Trevor."

"It's nice to meet you, Maya. Would you be interested in maybe having dinner sometime?"

"That sounds nice. Can I ask you a question?"

"Of course."

"I'm not shallow at all. This is coming from a conversation we were having before you came over. We were talking about cars. What men prefer, what women prefer, you know. Help us settle a debate we're having. What kind of car do you drive?"

"Me? Well, I have a Ford right now, but I'm about to get a...uh—"

"Trevor, stop. You have a Ford what?" Maya asks.

"A Ford Fiesta," he admits, putting his head down.

The women look at each other, struggling to hold back laughter.

"Well, Trevor, here's my card. Give me a call sometime," Maya says, with her same serious face.

"I will. What kind of car do you drive?" he asks.

"Oh, Trevor, I don't want to—"

"Fair is fair, Maya. You exposed me and my Fiesta. What are you pushing?"

"It's right in front of the restaurant. You can see it from the window here."

She hits the alarm button so he can see the four-door Porsche Turbo light up. Embarrassment fills Trevor's soul. He wants to just disappear, but he can't. He takes a big gulp and a deep breath and turns around to face the women. They are all holding in laughter, except for Maya, who never shows emotion. He tells them all to have a good evening and heads for the door.

"Are you proud of yourself?" asks Cian.

"I didn't do anything."

Quashon Davis

"You embarrassed that poor guy. He's gonna go home and cry," Tess laughs.

"He'll be okay," Maya says, maintaining her blank expression.

"Okay, girls, enough of her foolishness. Who's babysitting tomorrow?" asks Angie.

Tess raises her hand half-heartedly.

"Don't be like that. Raise that hand high," Cian demands.

"Whatever. I don't feel up to it."

"Well, it's your turn," says Maya.

"Fine."

"Now that we settled that, let's get the check and get out of here," says Angie.

***

Despite all the protesting from Captain Rayton, and after a long flight and a quick Uber ride, Roger Merrit walks into the police precinct that he once called home. All the officers stop what they're doing and stare at him in disbelief. He tries to act like he doesn't notice the fact that all eyes are on him. As he turns the corner to head for Rayton's office, he runs right into Pete. They stare at each other for a second, before Roger tries to speak.

"Pete, listen man. I'm…I just…I…"

"Roger, please…. You don't have to say anything. I understand why you shot me. I'm not mad. If you were trying to hurt me, you wouldn't have shot me in the vest. Welcome back," Pete says, extending his hand.

Roger shakes it, confused but relieved.

"You're alright with me, Raj. Good luck with the captain though. He's pretty pissed that you're back."

"Oh, I know he is."

SUSPECT BEHAVIOR

Roger walks into Captain Rayton's office with his head held high. He sits down nonchalantly while the captain stares at him in disbelief. They share thirty seconds of uncomfortable, tension-filled silence.

"Good to see you, Captain Rayton," Roger smiles.

"Well, it's not good to see you. If it was up to me, you would be rotting away in a cell at the bottom of Sing Sing. What you did was inexcusable. You shot a fellow officer, a former partner of yours, and left him lying in the street like a dog. How you can even live with yourself is a testament to how much of a bastard you are."

"He was coming out of my house after I figured out my wife was cheating. I shot him in the vest just to injure his ribs."

"And, was he the one that was sleeping with your wife?"

"No, he wasn't."

"So, the 'greatest detective ever' was wrong and because of that, a man was unfairly targeted."

"I apologized."

"And, you ran and hid for four years. You are a bastard, Merrit. I always knew it."

"Are you finished, Captain?"

"Why? You got something to say?"

"I do. The police are supposed to operate like a family. You held me back at every turn, did everything you could to make my job harder. For some reason, you were always bothered by how good I am at my job. I don't know why you hate me so much and I don't care. Stay out of my way and I'll stay out of yours."

"I knew you were an arrogant son of a bitch, but this takes the cake. After being a fugitive from justice for four years, you think you can just come in here and make demands? You're right. I never liked you. You made some high-profile arrests when you were a cop and the mayor was ready to adopt you.

Quashon Davis

You became a detective without even taking the exam. You were in the papers, on the news, everywhere. You thought you were bigger than this department."

"That's all, Rayton? You're jealous because I was the man here? You got a lotta nerve. I can't help that I'm good at what I do. You like following protocol. I like getting results. I won't apologize for that."

"Well, I know you have a case. The FBI was here earlier telling me about it."

"So, you know I'm goin' after The Ghost already."

"I sure do. That's why I assigned you a partner you're already familiar with."

"I don't need a partner, Rayton."

"That's *Captain* Rayton to you. And here, in this building, I make the decisions. I run this place. I say, if you're working for me, you're gonna have a partner."

"And, who would that be, *Captain* Rayton?" Merrit asks sarcastically.

"Why, your last partner of course, Marie. The two of you worked so well together. As the captain, I have to go with what works."

"Marie was the person my wife was having an affair with."

"Yeah, I think I did hear something about that. Actually, they're an official couple now. Make sure you congratulate her when the two of you ride over to interview Citronelli's family."

"I'm not riding over with Marie, and I'm not partnering up with her. She was sneaking behind my back and seeing my wife. She proved that she couldn't be trusted as a partner."

"No, Merrit, she had your back in the streets. She can't be trusted as a person maybe, but she's great as a partner."

"You're such a—"

SUSPECT BEHAVIOR

"If you wanna work here, you'll partner up with Marie. She's in a car out front. Enjoy your ride over to Citronelli's," laughs Rayton.

***

Marie is sitting in the unmarked car idling in front of the police station. She's sweating a little, and her hands are shaking. She would rather be anywhere else in the world right now. Roger was her partner, mentor, and friend. She not only had an affair with his wife, they've been a couple since Roger fled to Brazil. Marie was sure she would never see him again. But now, because of Rayton's hate for Roger, she's moments away from being in a car with the person she ultimately betrayed. Seconds feel like hours as she nervously waits for him to walk out of the precinct. For a moment, she considers pulling off, going home and not coming back. Before she can act on that thought, Roger makes his way out of the precinct, down the stairs and towards the car. He looks like he has worked out every day for the four years he's been gone. His beard is thick but perfectly shaped and his cold, dark brown eyes focus on Marie in the car and never move. He walks toward her with a heart full of anger and hate he didn't realize he had. The rage begins rising from his toes, and bubbles all the way to his brain. The sky appears to go from blue to dark gray in seconds. Marie sees him and can't move. She can't even open her mouth. Her tongue is glued to the bottom of it. All she can do is sit quietly while the man she destroyed walks up and gets into the car. He shuts the door and stares at her intently without saying a word. Fighting off the feeling of being overcome with nerves, Marie puts the car in drive and pulls off.

"So, full pardon, I see…" she says.

Roger doesn't say a word. He just continues to stare at her intensely.

"Must be nice to be back in the states again…"

Quashon Davis

Roger's silence has Marie on edge. She's trying not to show her uneasiness, but it's coming out. She almost rear-ends a car because she keeps glancing over. As she brings the car to a screeching halt, she looks over and there's Roger, still staring, not saying a word.

"You know what? You don't scare me, Roger. Yes, I was sleeping with Miesha behind your back. We're a couple now, have been since you left. We live in your old home. I play your damn Xbox. If you were doing the things you needed to do back then to keep her happy, maybe it wouldn't have happened. I'm not gonna apologize. If she was satisfied with you, she wouldn't have been open to being with me. I know you were her husband, but I made time and you didn't. I don't know what you want me to say. I don't know."

"Make a left at the light," he says.

Confused, Marie makes a left and tries to understand why he's still so mellow.

"Pull over here," he instructs.

"Where are we?" she asks.

They get out the car and go into a large studio. Roger leads the way as they get into an elevator and take it up to the top floor. The whole time, Marie continues to glance at him, making sure he doesn't try anything. The elevator doors open and there's Roger's friend, Jay.

"Raj! You made it," he says, hugging him.

"Yeah, man. Good to see you. Anyone else here?"

"Nope. I got you covered," Jay says, leading them to a large, dark room.

v many properties do you own, man?" asks Roger.

. This one I was gonna make into a dance studio, my gym away from home."

on the lights to reveal a boxing ring. He hands et . aır of gloves, then attempts to hand a pair to Marie.

17

"You must be kidding, right? I'm not fighting you. I'm not fighting a six foot eight, two-hundred-fifty-pound man," she says.

"Then, I'll keep hitting you until you do," he says, tightening up his gloves.

Marie begins to walk towards the door, but Jay steps in front of her. He's still holding the gloves out for her to take.

"You are out of your mind. You know what, me beating the hell out of you isn't gonna make Miesha love you again. You want some work, puta, you got it," she yells, snatching the gloves from Jay and putting them on. "I shoulda done this a long time ago," she says.

They climb in the ring and Jay stands on the outside.

"Anything you want me to do, Raj?"

"Make sure she doesn't die," Roger says with a stern look.

They circle each other slowly, each one intensely staring at the other. Marie doesn't waste time. She figures if she attacks first with speed and strength, she may be able to take him down and end this quickly. She rushes over and quickly pops Roger in his jaw twice with everything she has. She backs up and quickly realizes she's in big trouble. Roger is smiling. He begins to move towards her, slowly cutting the ring off, and backing her up into a corner. She throws three desperation punches that all land on Roger's face, and he brushes them off like nothing. He loads up and nails her in the stomach with a short punch. Marie grabs her stomach and bends forward in pain. Before she can recover, a quick uppercut puts her down on the canvas.

"Get up," Roger demands.

Marie slowly gets up. Roger comes toward her and she tries to surprise him and throws a kick out of desperation. He brushes her foot aside and hits her with a right hook to the side of her head that sends her down to the canvas again. Marie shakes her head, trying to get the cobwebs out.

Quashon Davis

"Get up," he demands.

"No," she says, still in a heap on the canvas.

"Get up."

"I've had enough."

"You were man enough to take my wife, right? You knew she was my high school sweetheart. You took advantage. As my partner, you knew we were going through a rough time and you used that knowledge to catch her slipping. Get up."

Marie hesitantly gets up. Jay climbs up on the ring apron, because he knows it's almost time to put a stop to this. Roger comes toward Marie and swings a quick jab that she ducks. Marie quickly kicks him on the side of his leg, sending him down to one knee. Before he can react, she clubs him on the side of his head with both fists, causing him to take a tumble. Jay's eyes open wide as he knows that shouldn't have happened. Roger smiles as he makes his way toward her one last time. Marie is starting to feel confident now: She sidesteps his jab and hits him twice in the shoulder. He swings again and she steps away. Finally, Roger fakes as if he's going to throw a punch and Marie steps away. When she looks up, she sees Roger's fist as the room goes completely dark.

CHAPTER TWO
A GHOST SIGHTING

MEANWHILE, **AT A BAR IN** the lobby of the Hotel Indigo, a woman sits patiently in the corner of the place, waiting with a big "Sunday-style" hat that covers most of her face. A man nervously walks up to her while she's waiting.

"Are you my contact?" he asks, looking around.

"That depends. Are you Tony?" she asks.

"I am."

"Good. You have something for me?"

"Listen, lady, the evidence I have on that guy is the kind of stuff that can get you killed. I shouldn't be out in public like this. They told me to lay low."

"Relax, Tony. No one knows you're here. It's fine. Tell me about the evidence you have."

"I have a drive. It has a video on it that would force him to resign immediately."

"Where is this drive?"

"In my pocket."

"Good. How much do you want for your drive, Tony?"

Quashon Davis

"I want ten million."

"Done. Was that so hard?" she asks.

"Really? That's it?"

"That's it. Let's drink to celebrate first, then I'll get your money," she says, handing him a glass.

He nervously looks at it for a second.

"It's poison, isn't it? Y-You're trying to poison me."

She calmly takes the glass back from him and quickly guzzles the drink until the glass is empty. She slides her drink over to him.

"I'm sorry, lady. I guess I'm a little paranoid. You can understand, right?" he asks, sipping the drink.

"I understand, Tony."

"I just can't be too careful right about now."

"I know. Let me see the drive."

"Let me see the money," he requests.

"I will get you your money. My people need some proof, Tony."

He takes another sip of his drink and pulls a small, silver thumb drive out of his pocket. He shows it to her and quickly stuffs it back into his pants.

"Excellent. Now we can do business."

***

As Marie's eyes slowly open and try to focus, she's confused as to why she's looking at the ceiling. It takes her a while to realize she's lying on her back. Her head is pounding. She sits up and tries to shake her senses back. As she begins to remember what happened, she looks over and sees Roger and Jay, sitting at a table having lunch. She climbs out of the ring, pissed, and walks toward them.

"You left me lying in that dirty-ass boxing ring while you had lunch? You got so much damn nerve," she says.

"No, Marie, you have the nerve. You got off easy though," Roger replies.

"What's that supposed to mean?"

"It means if you were a guy, I would've put some bullet holes in you."

"Yeah, whatever."

Roger's cell phone begins to ring. His mood stays low once he sees it's Captain Rayton.

"Yes, Captain?"

"There's a dead man at the Hotel Indigo."

"So?"

"His name is Tony Alves. He's a low-level informant, but recently, he's been bragging about having some information that was gonna set him up for life. Somebody didn't want that info getting out."

"I'm only supposed to be after The Ghost."

"We believe whoever that important person is that Tony had information on, hired The Ghost to take out any and everybody that came into contact with that information."

"You're saying The Ghost just assassinated this guy, Tony, in the lobby of a major hotel in broad daylight?"

"Yes."

"I'm on my way."

The Hotel Indigo has been a staple in the city for decades. The large lobby is known to have a celebrity or two, just sitting around reading a newspaper at any given time. Often, visiting sports teams use this as their hotel of choice. There are many things that make the Indigo great: the giant lobby with all its fine art and décor, the friendly wait staff, the widely popular chef, the large gym, even the parking deck. One thing it's never had to its credit, any type of crime. Unfortunately, that's no longer the case, as there's crime scene tape around the bar, and a dead body on the floor right by a stool. Cops are walking around, taking pictures and measurements, asking the patrons questions and looking for clues. Roger and Marie walk in. He does a quick scan before stopping one of the officers.

"Hey, what do you have?"

"Detective, it looks like the guy was poisoned. His name is Tony Alves. Doesn't really make sense though. Both glasses tested positive for poison, but the bartender said this guy had a drink with a woman, who we assume was the killer and they both drank. Both glasses tested positive for poison, so I'm not sure how she did it. She had to poison herself."

"You're thinking too much, young officer," Roger says, patting him on the back and looking at the glasses.

"Wait a minute, *you're* Roger Merrit. You're '*the*' Roger Merrit," he says.

"I am."

"Guys, it's Roger Merrit," he says loudly.

The other officers stop what they're doing and come over to meet Roger. The young cops are all in awe of the iconic detective.

"I was under the impression I wouldn't be accepted by the other guys when I came back," Roger admits.

"Are you kidding? We all know the story. The captain's always messing with you, your ex-wife, the…" they all stop and look over at Marie.

"But, she…she's the one that—"

"We've got work to concentrate on, young fella. What's your name?"

"Spencer, sir. Daniel Spencer."

"Okay, Spencer. What exactly did the bartender say?"

"He said the dead guy was sitting here talking to a woman. There are cameras in here, but they aren't working. They both had drinks in those two glasses. Both glasses have remnants of poison in them. She had to poison herself as well."

"If she poisoned herself, where is she, Spencer?"

"I don't know, Detective. It doesn't make sense."

"Spencer, get out of his way. Just let the man do his thing," one of the other officers says.

All of the young cops cheer in agreement, while Marie stands in the corner annoyed. Roger carefully examines the glasses. He looks around the room, comes back to the glasses again, and smiles.

The Ghost is good, he thinks.

"Okay, so the bartender told you that Tony and the killer both drank from these two glasses, correct?" asks Roger.

"Yes, sir."

"You tested both glasses and they both had poison in them, correct?"

"Yes, sir."

"So, how could both of them have drunk poison, and only one person is dead on the floor?"

"I don't know, Detective."

"Anyone?" Roger asks.

The silent room has no ideas or answers for him. They are hanging off his every word.

"Officer Spencer, do you notice any differences in the two glasses?" he asks.

"No, sir."

"Look a little closer."

"Uh, one of them has a little bit of water in it."

"Okay, does that ring a bell at all?"

"No, sir."

"It should. If you, or any of you, ever plan on passing the detective's exam one day, remember to always notice everything. Always think out of the box. One glass has a little bit of water on the bottom, the other one doesn't. What would cause water in the bottom of a drinking glass?"

"Ice?" asks Spencer.

"Yes, ice. If they were having the same drink, why would there be water from ice left behind in one glass, but not the other?"

"One person drank quickly?"

"Yes. The killer must've poisoned the ice cubes. She drank her drink quickly before the ice melted. The victim didn't know he was being poisoned. He took his time drinking and the poisoned ice cubes melted into his drink. Find out everything you can on the type of poison. See if any camera in this building got a glimpse of this woman."

"Right away, Detective Merrit," Spencer says, rushing off.

The other officers stand around amazed, staring at Roger.

"Poisoned ice cubes? This guy is incredible," one of the officers proclaims.

As Roger makes a few quick notes on his pad, he begins to walk. Marie slowly catches up to him.

"I see you still haven't lost your touch."

He stares at her again without saying a word.

"You know, this is getting old. At some point, you're gonna hafta let this go, otherwise we can't work together," she says.

"I agree. We can't. I don't want or need your help. I'm gonna take down The Ghost alone."

"What about me? The captain said I had to partner with you."

SUSPECT BEHAVIOR

"Go home to my wife. I'll take care of it," he says as he gets in the car and speeds away, leaving Marie to fend for herself.

***

Meanwhile, at a small church in an upscale section of the city, Jay is walking in to pick up his son, James. He's only four years old, but he's clearly going to be a star. Jay always hoped he'd have a son to follow in his footsteps and become a star athlete, but James is clearly already on a different path. As he walks into the church's after-care program, all of the adults and children are crowded around James, as he plays the piano almost flawlessly. The four-year-old then has the nerve to sing classic Jackson Five. The adults have their phones out, recording in utter disbelief. The last thing Jay wants is for any of this going public. He walks over to the piano and calmly grabs James by the arm.

"It's time to go home, son."

Everyone sighs with disapproval as Jay takes him away before he can finish his rendition.

"Mr. Jones. Are you in a hurry?" asks one of the camp counselors.

"Kind of."

"Well, I won't keep you. James has amazing gifts. He's going to be a star. No one that young should be able to sing like that, much less play the piano. He's truly amazing. I know he goes to that fancy arts school. I have a friend that works for Channel 7. I was hoping maybe we could show her what he can do. Maybe get him on the news? If that's okay?"

"I appreciate that. You know, I haven't been retired that long, and we're trying to move away from the spotlight. If that happened, it would start up all over again. I still get a ton of attention everywhere I go, but we want James to be low-key. I appreciate the offer, but we're gonna keep him out of the spotlight as long as we can."

"I understand completely. Have a nice day, okay?"

"Thanks. You do the same."

As Jay walks his son out of the church, he takes a deep breath.

"Didn't I tell you not to sing and entertain people?" he asks.

"Sorry, Daddy."

Inside the church, in the last pew, deep in the corner, a woman sits to herself. She watched the entire performance. She's caught it a couple of times. She has a big pair of shades on, and her hair is wrapped in a scarf. She sits for a few more minutes, before quietly making her way out the church.

"That woman looks familiar," says one of the counselors.

Before they can figure out who she is, her black Ferrari rumbles away in a cloud of dust.

***

The Dirty Circle, a tiny bar that has survived the test of time, sits on one of the few desolate streets in the middle of midtown. The bartender, Train, is a third-generation owner of the place. His real name is Lonnie, but he's gone by the name Train since he was a kid. Growing up, he never had an interest in riding a bike or catching a bus anywhere. He only rode the trains, hence the nickname. To this day, at fifty-five years old, he's never had a driver's license. Train has been in the city so long, he knows a little bit of everybody and for some reason, knows a little bit of everything.

Roger walks into the bar and smiles wide as he sits down on one of the old stools.

"Train, good to see you, bro," he says.

"Roger Merrit, I heard you were back. It's good to see you. How was Brazil?"

"Train, you never cease to amaze me. How'd you know I was back?"

"Come on, Raj. You know I got my ways. You want the usual?"

"I'm on the clock. Gimme a Sprite with no ice."

"Ha! You're gettin' soft in your old age, Detective," Train says, pouring the Sprite from the tap.

He places it down in front of Roger, and then pours himself a shot of Hennessy.

"To healthy returns," he says, tapping his glass against Roger's.

"Do you know why they reinstated me?"

"You got me with that one, Raj."

"They want me to catch The Ghost."

"Oh, God…"

"I can catch her, Train."

"Like last time? That woman almost killed you. Didn't you hafta go to therapy after you tried before?"

"This is gonna be different."

"How, Raj? How's it gonna be different?"

"You just gotta trust me. I'm gonna catch her this time."

"No, she's gonna kill you. Let somebody else get her."

"Train, you don't believe in me? Come on."

"I can't lie to you. I've known you since you were in high school. You got that scholarship to play football at Michigan and you swore you were going pro. Do you remember what I told you before you left for college?"

"You said I wasn't gonna play pro football. I was gonna end up doing some kind of law enforcement."

Quashon Davis

"Exactly. I know what I'm talkin about, Raj. The Ghost has kills all around the globe. She'll kill you, Raj. I don't wanna see that happen. You're smart as hell, and you're a great detective. Hell, you're one of the best. The Ghost is better. I'm sorry."

"What have you heard? I know you know something."

"There's a drive. It has something on it that would change a whole lot of things. Word on the street is, it's worth any amount of money. Well, whoever it has information on must be pretty important, 'cause they hired the ghost at eight million per kill to eliminate anyone who's seen or handled it."

"How do you know all that?"

"Don't worry about it. Are you gonna take my advice and leave The Ghost alone?"

"No, Train, I'm gonna do my job," he says, taking a swig of his Sprite. "Thanks for believing in me," he adds as he walks out the bar.

***

He gets into his car and before he can pull off, the phone rings. After a long sigh, it takes the big man a few seconds to maneuver to the point where he can take his phone out of his pocket.

"Jay? What's up bro?" he asks.

"Raj, I need to talk to you."

"What's wrong? You don't sound good."

"I gotta tell you something, Raj. It's not good. I did a bad thing. I-I never got the chance to tell you about it."

"You talk to me every week. What do you mean, you never had the chance?"

"It's bad, Raj."

"Okay, tell me."

29

"I was stuck in a corner, man. I didn't know what to do. Sapphire was pregnant. Shel was pregnant. I didn't want to tell Shel. I didn't want the media to find out about Sapphire. It would've been a damn circus."

"Well, you got lucky. Sapphire miscarried and Shel didn't. Problem solved. I remember."

"Raj, it was the other way around."

"What are you talking about, Jay?"

"Shel miscarried. Sapphire didn't."

"What are you talkin' about? Shel had the baby. James is...oh damn, Jay. You gotta be kidding, man."

"Yeah, Raj."

"What did you do? Pay the doctor?"

"Yeah. Shel miscarried and since Sapphire had to be under when she gave birth, I paid him to tell her that she was the one that miscarried."

"How much did that cost you?"

"Fifty grand."

"So, you and Shel have this kid that isn't hers. Does Shel know?"

"No."

"Are you crazy? Why are you even telling me this, bro?"

"You're my best friend. I've kept this to myself for four years. I had to tell you."

"No, you didn't, Jay. I'm a detective. My job is to uphold the law. I don't wanna know this. We need to act like I didn't hear anything."

"No, Raj. When you needed help, I was there for you. You needed to get outta the country quick and I made it happen. If it wasn't for me, you woulda been in jail these last few years."

"Okay, that's actually true."

Quashon Davis

"I know it is. The boy isn't even five years old yet and he's playing the piano and singing like he's Ray Charles. People are starting to notice. When I went to pick him up from daycare the other day, I could've sworn I saw one of Sapphire's cars in the parking lot."

"Oh, damn."

"I don't know what to do."

"Jay, the only thing you can do is tell the truth. The lie is breaking down. She's gonna find out eventually, bro. Maybe you can just tell her."

"Are you kidding, Raj? Tell her that I faked the death of her child and I've been raising him with my *wife*? Tell my wife that her child was stillborn, and the one she's been raising is from me sneaking around with someone else?"

"Okay, when you say it like that, it just sounds really bad. I don't know what you can do though. Damn, Jay, that wasn't a good plan at all."

"I know."

"I really don't wanna be involved in that. I know you're my boy and I owe you a lot, so I'll look the other way, but there's not much I can do."

"Raj, you gotta help me think of something."

"I'll see what I can come up with. In the meantime, maybe you should try to get out ahead of this."

"How, Raj?"

"Maybe you should talk to Sapphire."

"What? Why?"

"You said you thought you saw her car. Maybe she already knows. You might be able to reason with her."

"That's a last resort, Raj."

"You may get to that point sooner than you think."

CHAPTER THREE
D & D SPORTS AGENCY

IN MADISON SQUARE GARDEN, THE country's most famous arena, it's one of the most exciting events of the summer, the NFL draft. For the whole week, the city is flooded with young, soon-to-be rookies. Some have been taking in the sights and taking it easy, while others have been partying hard. Its midnight on the eve of the draft, and at Club R & B's, a lot of the soon-to-be draftees are enjoying one last night of partying. In the VIP section, the Heisman Trophy winner, Miles Greenway, is popping bottles with his friends; Alabama's Will Upshaw, and LSU's Jodie Simpson. They're surrounded by women they don't know, who are working hard to get close to them in anticipation of them getting drafted.

"This weeks been crazy," says Miles.

"Hell, yeah. I wonder how many babies I made this week," adds Jodie.

Will pours champagne while staring at Jodie like he's crazy.

"I hope you're kidding, bro. You're not even in the league yet."

"Hell no, I'm not kidding. I been putting it down all week."

"You crazy as hell. Soon as you get that first NFL paycheck, you gonna be paying for kids you never see from chicks you don't know. What are you doin'?" Miles asks.

"That's how we do it in Louisiana. Get it first, ask questions later."

A man walks into the VIP section. The short, dark-skinned guy puts his glasses in his jacket pocket.

"Hey, Dante. Over here, bro," Miles says, standing up. "Fellas, this is my agent, Dante Sproles."

They greet him as he sits down and pulls out his iPad.

"Fellas, I know the draft is tomorrow night. Miles tells me neither one of you has an agent yet. Because of my reputation, I didn't go to Miles. He came to me and asked if I would be his agent."

"Do you represent anyone we've heard of?" asks Will.

"You ever heard of Jay Jones?"

"*The* Jay Jones? The king of New York?" they ask with widened eyes.

"Yes, he's one of my clients. My company does great things. I mean, listen. I'll get you the biggest contract I can, but it's the other services I provide that make me the best agent there is."

"Other services?" Will and Jodie ask.

"My brother, Damon, handles the 'other services.' We protect our clients at *all* costs. When you sign with us, we make sure you stay out of trouble."

"What do you mean?" asks Will.

"Damon has a small team, a computer expert, a fixer, a doctor, and a talker. They make sure whatever situation you get in, they get you out and keep you clean."

"We don't need all that," says Jodie.

"Every young athlete needs all that," Dante rebuts.

"What's your fee for signing with you?" asks Will.

"I get fifteen percent."

"What? Every agent we talked to charges five to ten percent," Jodie says.

"Every agent doesn't do what I do."

"Fellas, you need this guy in your corner, trust me. I signed with him as soon as I graduated," says Miles.

"I ain't givin' up that much money. I expect my contract to be at least three million. I don't know what fifteen percent of that is, but I know it's too much. You really signed with this guy for fifteen percent of your money?" asks Jodie.

"Hell yeah," Miles replies.

"Why?"

"Cause I like to drink and have a good time. This dude, Dante, ain't just an agent. He keeps these chicks from taking advantage of you. He keeps you outta trouble. I talked with dudes around the league and they say he's the guy to sign with."

"Naw, man, I think I'm good. I appreciate you coming down here, but I'm gonna take my chances with a cheaper agent," Will says.

"Yeah, me too," adds Jodie.

"Fellas, I wish you the best of luck. Here's my card if you change your mind. Let me warn you though, if you try to acquire my services once you get into trouble, my fee goes up to twenty percent."

They both begin to laugh as Dante buttons up his coat and walks away. More women come over to sit with the young athletes in their section.

"I can't believe that's your agent, Miles. He's ripping you off," Jodie says.

"No, he's not. But, he's gonna rip you off when you sign with him for twenty percent."

"We're not doing that," says Will.

"I partied with you two all week. You need him. You'll be begging him to take your twenty percent. Mark my words."

***

The next morning, Dante walks into his office with his briefcase in one hand, and his coffee in the other. He greets the elevator attendant and rides up to the top floor. As he walks into D & D Sports Management, he's greeted by his business partner and childhood friend, Damon. Who, like most mornings, is sitting with his feet up.

"You lazy bastard," Dante says.

"It's eight am, what do you want from me, bro?"

"Yeah, whatever. Did you see that Hawks game last night?"

"I saw it. Where's my coffee?"

"I'm not carrying two cups of coffee. Why I gotta tell you that every day?"

"Anyway, I hear Smith Jr. just got a hundred and fifty-million-dollar sneaker deal."

"Hell yeah, Damon. Another fifteen mil for this company. Where is everybody?"

"In your office. You get to tell them how busy these next few weeks are gonna be."

"Let's go," Dante says, walking towards his office.

He throws the door open and looks over his tired team.

"Good morning, everyone. I know you all are tired. We've been busy. I could lie to you and tell you that business is gonna slow down, but it's not. As you know, we just hired Joe here, who's gonna be our doctor. Basically, if a client calls us with an emergency that needs to be fixed off the books, Joe will go and take care of it. Welcome, Joe. As we expand, we're…"

Dante's phone begins to ring.

"One minute, team. Hello?"

"Yo, Dante, it's Miles. We messed up bad, man."

"What happened?"

"After the club, we took these girls up to our room. We had sex. One of them keeps saying we raped her."

"Okay, calm down, Miles."

"I can't calm the hell down. The draft is today."

"Are the girls still in your hotel room?"

"Yeah. This chick is on the phone with the cops right now."

"You got drugs in there?"

"Just weed."

"Damon will be there in five minutes. He'll take care of it. In the meantime, get all the weed you got in there together and give it to him when he gets there."

"Okay, thanks, man. I'm scared as hell," Miles admits.

Dante disconnects the call. "That was our Heisman Trophy winning, top draft pick. Him and his boys are about to go down for rape."

"Did they do it?" asks Damon.

"Doesn't matter. He's our client. The girl is on the phone with the cops already. Their normal response time is ten minutes. Get over there in five."

"Okay, I'll take care of it," says Damon.

"Take R.J. with you."

"Come on, Dante. I don't need that young punk. You know how annoying he is."

Quashon Davis

"Ummm...you know I'm sitting right here, right?" asks R.J.

"Shut up, man. You know you're annoying. It ain't no secret," Damon says.

"You just don't like young people. You're mad 'cause you're old."

"Old? I'm thirty-one."

"Exactly. I'm twenty-one. I'm a computer expert, with the same money you got, and I'm taller."

"You don't have more money than me, you punk."

"Fellas! The cops will be there in less than ten minutes. You better be there in five," Dante orders.

"Alright, fine. Let's go, youngster," Damon says.

"Cool, but I'm driving," says R.J.

"Come on, man, I'm the one with the Benz."

"And, I got the Lexus."

"You tryin' to say that crappy Lexus is better than my Benz?"

"Please, you can't mess with my whip."

"You don't—" Damon starts before being cut off.

"Would you two shut up and get over to the hotel?" Dante shouts.

"Damn, boss, sip on that decaf, we'll be back," says R.J.

As the door closes, Dante takes a big sip.

"We're gonna be pretty busy these next few weeks. I hope you all are ready. Veronica keep that attitude in check, okay?"

"I don't have an attitude."

"Yes, you do, Ronnie."

"I said, I don't. Don't make me punch you in the mouth."

"Good to know you don't have an attitude this morning," says Dante.

"Shut up," she responds.

He continues. "Joe, you're gonna be especially busy. With the draft tomorrow, there's a flock of young, idiot rookies flooding the city. They're gonna get into all types of trouble. A lot of them are gonna get hurt, or hurt people. The kinds of hurt we'll need to keep from being recorded."

"I understand," says Joe.

"Veronica, you'll be handling all of the dirty work."

"It's Ronnie, you short bastard."

Everyone giggles as Dante continues. "Yeah...love the energy. Dre, you'll be doing a lot of talking. You know you're the first point of contact, ninety percent of the time."

"I'm good, boss. I'm always ready to talk."

"We know that," Ronnie says.

"Anyway, Dante, shouldn't you have went with them?" asks Dre.

"For what?"

" 'Cause they don't like each other."

"Don't worry about that. Damon and R.J. are more alike than they realize. And they're both good at what they do."

***

The two men enter the hotel. They're clearly in a hurry as they speed-walk past the reception desk toward the elevators.

"I can't even think straight because of that loud trash you were blasting in the car," says Damon.

"You old guys complain about everything. How can you call Migos trash? Why are you so miserable?"

"Why do you keep saying that? I'm in my early thirties, that's young."

"Naw man, I'm young. You're like, somebody's great uncle or something."

Quashon Davis

"You never make sense when you talk. Maybe that's a younger generation thing."

"Damon, you wanna be twenty-one again, hella bad."

"Whatever, R.J., listen…when we get inside, let me do all the talking."

"I know the drill. I gotchu."

They knock on the door. Miles answers, clearly nervous.

"Damon, thank God. Come in, come in. The girls called the cops already."

Will and Jodie are quietly sitting at the table. The three girls are sitting on the couch, two of them consoling the one that's crying.

"Before I start, I only have Miles listed here as one of our clients. I take it you two gentlemen would now like to be represented by D & D?" Damon asks.

"Yes," Will and Jodie yell.

"That's gonna be at a rate of twenty percent."

"Fine, whatever," they both agree.

He quickly has them sign contracts on his iPad. While they're signing, Miles hands him a bag of weed.

"Okay ladies, tell me what happened," Damon says.

"You'll find out when the cops get here," one of the girls says.

"Don't say anything," another chimes in.

"What's your name?" he asks the crying girl.

She ignores him, looking away.

"Her name is Andrea, Andrea Hawkins," Jodie blurts out.

R.J. quickly opens his laptop and begins typing feverishly.

"You've got less than four minutes," Damon says.

"Be easy, old school. I only need two."

"I'm not old. Anyway, Andrea, are you claiming you were raped? What exactly happened?"

"She's not *claiming* anything. She *was* raped," one of the girls says angrily.

"And who raped you?"

"They...all did..." she whispers through her tears.

R.J. turns the laptop towards Damon and gives him a head nod.

"I can't have this," Miles shouts.

"You only got about a minute, old man," R.J. warns.

"According to what I'm looking at here, Ms. Hawkins, you just finished your first year of law school."

"So?" she whispers.

"Well, you scored a one-eighty on your LSAT," adds Damon.

"So?"

He continues, "So, you took the practice test five times. You got a one-twenty each time. That's pretty low. The average score is one-fifty. You were well below average, Ms. Hawkins. You weren't really law school material, but your jump to one-eighty allowed you to get into Columbia."

"What is your point?" one of her friends asks.

"My point is that no one jumps that high. You were a C-student in college. Now, your sister on the other hand, she was a straight-A student. According to this, you took the exam on May first of 2016 at NYU. Now, if we pull up the security footage from that day, are we gonna see you? Or, are we gonna see your sister?"

"You bastard," one of the girls says.

"Open the door. Police," a voice says, while banging on the door.

Quashon Davis

"I'd hate to see you throw away your law career before it gets started."

"Don't listen to him. Tell the police what happened," one of the girls says.

Jodie opens the door and two cops walk in.

"Who's Andrea Hawkins?" one of them says.

"I am. I wasn't raped. I didn't mean to say that. I was upset and I wasn't thinking clearly."

"Ma'am, are you sure?"

"Yes."

"If you change your mind, call us."

As the officers walk out, a third is waiting on the stairs.

"What happened?" he asks.

"She recanted. Said she wasn't raped."

"Why?"

"Damon Johnson is in there."

"Dammit...one day we're gonna bring down D & D Sports Management. I wanna burn that company to the ground, and I want those bastards locked up."

"You really hate them, huh?"

"They're dirty. They cover up whatever crap their so-called *clients* do wrong."

"Morning, Officers," Damon says as he and R.J. walk out of the hotel.

"Let me guess, you got that poor, young rape victim to change her mind and say she wasn't raped? Your 'client' is more important than the life of that girl. You're criminals."

"Officer Reyes...it's always a pleasure to see you. At D & D, our clients are indeed of the utmost importance to us. We just came by to speak with them about the draft today."

41

"That's bullshit. I'm not stupid. Let me tell you something. You and your little crew are gonna get sloppy. Eventually, you're gonna end up in a situation you can't fix. When you do, I'll be waiting,"

"That's very ambitious, Officer Reyes. I understand, but we're just sports agents."

The officers angrily watch them get into their car and pull off.

***

"Security cameras? You were really reaching with that one," says R.J.

"She didn't know that. We got the job done," Damon replies.

"You ever think what we're doing is wrong?" R.J. asks.

"No. We do a job and that's it. Don't get all heady about it,"

"Reyes is always right on our heels. He might've had a point this time. Don't you think that girl was raped?"

"I never thought about it. Our client was in trouble. That was my only concern. And you know what? It should've been your only concern too."

"Okay, Damon, never mind."

"Look, you're young, and you're making more money than most people. We're not murderers or drug dealers. We do a job, no more, no less. We do what needs to be done to protect our clients. That's the job."

"But, we're not robots. We know right from wrong."

"Look, ten years ago, me and Dante were two high school dropouts living on the streets. We were robbing people just to get by. Jay Jones came along and gave us an opportunity. We became his agent and trainer and people took notice. The rest is history."

Quashon Davis

"History, huh?"

"That's right. Jay was in trouble once, so we had to fix a situation for him. Nothing major, we just had to cause a young woman to have a minor traffic accident. After that, we started going that extra mile helping all of our clients. Word spread that D & D Sports Management did whatever they had to do to protect their clients."

"So?"

"So, do you like your car, R.J.?"

"Of course, I do."

"And that nice big brownstone you have, with the view?"

"Yeah."

"Then, stop thinking of this as anything but a job. When you start thinking, bad things happen. The rest of us get nervous."

"I'm no rat."

"Then you damn well better not start smelling like one."

***

Joe, the newly hired on-call doctor for D & D is heading to his first call. He was once one of the top doctors in the country, but his fall from grace was quick and permanent. He was once a hard-working, married father of two young girls, but Joe's money and fame began to get the better of him. One night at a high society party, he discovered cocaine. It quickly tore him down, draining his bank accounts, ruining his marriage and hurting his relationship with his kids. He's now divorced, bouncing in and out of court in attempts to try and get whatever visitation he can. Before his downfall, Joe's exploits were the stuff legends are made of. He once rescued a man who was in cardiac arrest at a restaurant, with nothing but a butter knife and a straw. Nowadays, those stories are old folk tales no one cares about. After months of struggling through life with no real income, just performing back alley stitches and light procedures for cash, he was approached by D & D, and immediately hired. Thrilled to be on the payroll for the top sports firm in the business right now, Joe is determined to put his best foot forward. He walks up to the home of Jack Bixby, offensive lineman for the New York Jets. He rings the doorbell while taking a quick look around. The door opens, and the giant offensive lineman fills the entire doorway. He looks Joe up and down with a disrespectful look, and steps aside so he can come in.

"What took you so long? She's in the living room," says Bixby.

Joe nods his head and walks into the giant home. As he enters the main area, there's a woman on the floor crying. She's holding her arm, which is clearly broken. Joe is instantly upset. He knows the motto of his new employer, and his first outing is already a test.

"Let me take a look. Your arm is definitely broken. I'm gonna give you something for the pain. It's not poking out of the skin, so I can set it and well, put a cast on it. You'll be good as new in a few weeks. How did it happen?"

She looks up at the massive Bixby, who gives her the "I dare you" look.

"I fell down all those stairs," she says.

"Just do your damn job, quack," Bixby demands.

"Fine. I'm gonna need eighty-five hundred dollars cash from you."

"Shit! That's a lot of damn money!"

"If you take her to a hospital, it would be a lot more, literally and figuratively."

"You got a mouth on you, Doc," Bixby says, opening his safe.

Quashon Davis

He takes out a few stacks of money and puts them on the table.

"When you're done, take her with you. There's a bus stop at the corner," Bixby says, walking up the stairs to his bedroom.

Joe is pissed. He knows he's in trouble with this job. Damon and Dante warned him several times about checking all emotions at the door when it comes to working for D & D. As he continues to work on her while she cries, Joe knows he may have taken a position he can't handle. He takes out his phone to call his boss.

"Hey, Joe, what was the deal? You good?"

"Dante, I don't know if I can do this, man. This guy…client…Jack Bixby, broke a woman's arm. I'm working on her now, but this is a lot. I don't know if—"

"Hey Joe, no need to explain, my man. This job isn't for everyone. I completely understand. When you finish with the young lady, come on back and we can settle up. I mean, you figure if you charged eighty-five hundred for that house call, we take five, you keep the rest. You would have at least ten house calls a week. I'm no mathematician, but I think that's about thirty-five G's a week."

"I guess I can try for a little while and see how it works out."

"That's the spirit, Joe. When you're done there, I need you to head uptown. We got a young client that thinks he took some bad drugs. I'll send you the address."

"Ok…"

***

Maya is just finishing up her workout at the gym. She's tired, and her yoga pants are causing all kinds of trouble. As she walks past the indoor basketball court to get a drink of water from the fountain, the men all stop playing and stare at her uncomfortably. As usual, Maya doesn't show any emotion whatsoever as she quickly gets her drink and heads for the locker room. Just before she walks in to shower and change, she notices a man getting information at the front desk. Even though her workout was vigorous, she quickly feels a burst of energy. *This man has to be six foot eight. His shoulders go on for days, and his beard looks like it was sculpted by Da Vinci himself.* Maya is beyond intrigued, as she walks over pretending to need a spare locker key. The man is filling out an application at the counter.

"You joining the gym?" she asks.

"I think so," he replies, without looking up.

"Cool. It's a nice gym. There's a lot of space. Classes are good. The price isn't too bad either."

"Yeah, I noticed that." He looks up and sees Maya's tall curvaceous frame. It goes on and on. Her pretty face captivates him. All of a sudden, he's nervous.

"I, um…I…yeah, the gym seems nice," he stumbles.

"It is. I'm Maya, Maya Ford."

"Roger Merrit."

"Nice to meet you, Roger."

"Nice to meet you, Maya."

She wants to smile, but she doesn't know how. Instead, she just keeps her intense serious look. She wants to make a joke, but she can't. She doesn't do that either.

"Well, Roger, maybe I can show you around the gym once you're a member."

"That sounds nice. Maybe we can have dinner sometime," he suggests.

"Dinner? When would you be trying to do that?"

"I'll wait for you to get out of the shower," he says, sitting down.

Quashon Davis

Maya looks to the side as she felt a tingle when he smoothly laid down that line. Maya doesn't feel tingles. She shrugs it off quickly.

"Smooth, Roger. If you don't mind me being dressed down, I can definitely eat."

"I don't mind at all."

"Then, I'll be right back."

CHAPTER FOUR
DIVIDE AND CONQUER

AFTER A LONG DAY, R.J. pulls into the garage of his brownstone. The twenty-one-year-old is living the dream. He owns a large home in the nice, Park Slope section of Brooklyn, drives a nice car, and has a plethora of women that he spends time with. The main one, Dez, is already at his home waiting for him. She doesn't have a key, but the tech-savvy R.J. controls his locks with his phone. Dez has been inside for a couple of hours, getting his dinner together. She wants a key, but because she knows what a great catch R.J. is, she doesn't say or do anything to put pressure on him. He's only twenty-one, but he's making six figures and he's smart. Dez is three years older than R.J., a senior at NYU, and student loans are killing her. She knows if she can beat out the other women R.J. spends time with, she can get those student loans paid. She cares about him, but seventy-four thousand dollars in debt is a lot. She knows if she can make him her man, it becomes "their" debt, and he'll take care of most of it.

R.J. struggled a little today, feeling conflicted. He gets out of his car and sees someone standing in his driveway. He grabs his computer bag and walks out to see Officer Reyes waiting for him.

"I don't have anything to say to you," R.J. says.

Quashon Davis

"Good, I'll do the talking then," says Reyes.

R.J. tries to walk past him, but Reyes lightly grabs his shirt.

"The girl that was raped, you got her to recant. How'd you do it?"

"I don't know what you're talkin' about."

"Here's the thing, R.J., D & D is going down. These 'situations' that you guys fix, is gonna eventually blow up in your face. You can't keep this up. We're onto you. Listen, you're twenty-one years old, this place had to cost four hundred grand at least. You got a nice ride. You really want to go to jail until you're forty-one years old? Talk to me, tell me everything you know, and I'll make sure you have total immunity when we take your bosses down. I promise. Listen, they're goin' down. You just need to decide if you're goin' down with them."

"I don't know what you're talkin' about, Reyes. I'm a sports agent. I represent clients of D & D. That's all I have to say."

"Okay, have it your way. If you change your mind, I know that they keep a ledger that lists all of the situations you guys have 'fixed.' If you give it to us, we'll make sure you stay outta jail. Think about it, kid, ain't no tech in prison."

Reyes gets into his squad car and pulls off slowly. R.J. watches him intensely as he walks into his house.

"What was that about?" Dez says, kissing him.

"Nothin', cops always gotta be cops. They don't have a clue, so they try to get information. It was nothing."

"You look worried. You know you can talk to me, R.J."

"I'm good. I just need time to think."

"Shouldn't you call your bosses and tell them that cop came by, harassing you?"

"Dez, you gotta leave me alone, okay? I'll handle it."

49

"I'm sorry. I'm just concerned. That cop coming to your home like that is unacceptable. I just think you should tell your bosses right away."

"Thanks for your opinion."

"R.J., you're not thinking about selling out your company, are you?"

"Dez, don't you have some dinner to finish? Let me handle this."

Dez reluctantly walks back into the kitchen. R.J. picks up his phone and thinks about dialing Dante or Damon. After staring at their names for several minutes, he puts the phone back down on the table and turns on the television.

***

At a small diner in the city, Roger and Maya are having dinner. The detective in him has a lot of questions as to why she seems almost like a robot. Her beauty and straightforwardness intrigue him, nevertheless. Roger can't stop staring at her.

Maya lives to say "no thank you," to men. She never shows interest in anyone, and her facial expression probably hasn't changed since the eighth grade. Although she knows when a man is handsome, she just can't show emotion or feelings. Roger seems to intrigue her just a little more than usual.

"So, Maya, what do you do for a living?"

"I'm a dentist."

"Really? That's interesting. Do you like it?"

"Not really. It's a living. I was in the Army and I did my time. When I got out, I went to school for teeth. Next thing you know, I was a dentist."

"You were in the Army? Wow, that's interesting. What was your rank?"

Quashon Davis

"I was a sergeant. I was deployed twice to Iraq, once in 2003, and again in 2005. I was home for good in 2007. I graduated from Georgetown School of Medicine in 2012. I started my own business and never looked back,"

"That's fantastic. What was it like in Iraq? Were you scared?"

"It was war. I wasn't scared at all. I prepared for war from the day I enlisted. My male counterparts couldn't understand why I rose up the ranks ahead of them. To answer your question though, it was death everywhere. There wasn't a moment where you could ever let your guard down. I saw people get sniped while they were sleeping, peeing, even eating their dinner. Mines, suicide drivers, kids with automatic weapons, it was an experience I'll never forget,"

"Wow, and you made it in and out of there twice?"

"I did."

"That's amazing,"

"I guess. What do you do, Roger?"

"I'm a detective here in the city."

"Really? That sounds interesting. You must have a ton of stories."

"Ah, not really. I've seen a few things, just like you have."

"I'm sure you have. Are you working on anything interesting right now?"

"I am, actually. I can't really talk about it, though."

"I understand."

"Maya, I have yet to see you smile. You're a beautiful woman. Is there a reason you don't smile? Are you like the Kardashians or something? I heard they don't smile because they think it keeps them from getting wrinkles."

"That's funny, Roger. I had a rough childhood. My dad was in the Army and we traveled all around the world constantly. He was abusive to my mother and me. He would

51

ask me what I was so happy for if I was smiling whenever I came home from school, or outside, or anywhere. Then, he would beat me and my mom. Finally, I just stopped smiling so we wouldn't get beat. That went on for years. When I turned eighteen, I got my acceptance letter to the Army. I was so happy, I couldn't hide it. I read the letter in front of them and I smiled. He proceeded to beat me for being happy. He always said, 'Happiness is an emotion a real soldier can't have.' He turned to my mother and pushed her down the stairs, breaking her neck. He stood at the top of the stairs and stared down at her for at least five minutes. He turned and looked at me, pulled out his service revolver and told me, 'Happiness is overrated,' before he blew his brains out. I buried them both, left for the Army, and I haven't smiled since."

"Um…I'm not really sure what to say to that. I should've just asked some traditional date questions like, what kinda music you like? Your favorite ice cream, stuff like that. I'm sorry. No one should have to go through that. As bad as that was though, you can't torture yourself by never smiling again."

"I'm not torturing myself. This is who I am. Those events made me Maya. Would I go back and change them if I could? Of course I would. I can't though. Everything happens for a reason. I'm much stronger for it. I love who I am. I've experienced more things and been to more places, than most people will ever see in their lifetime. I'm grateful for that."

"When you're happy about something, how do you express it?"

"I don't."

"If a man satisfies you, how does he know he did?"

"I let him do it again."

"So, if you're at a movie and something funny happens, you don't laugh?"

"No."

"That's interesting."

Quashon Davis

"I guess so."

***

Joe pulls into the parking lot of his apartment building, exhausted. He turned in the office's portion of his pay and he sits in his car, counting his cash. He made three stops today. Each one was an eighty-five-hundred-dollar charge, with five grand going to D & D.

"Ten thousand, five hundred bucks in one day," he says to himself.

He gets out of his car, excited. He can't wait to move out of his crappy apartment. As he walks toward his door, he sees an unfamiliar face standing in front of a cop car.

"Hi, Joe," the man says.

"Do I know you?"

"Not yet, but I know you. Joseph Mickens, former doctor to the stars. You used to be famous. I remember seeing you on television. You got caught up with cocaine, and you fell hard. I remember you did some time."

"Who are you?"

"The name's Reyes, Officer Reyes. You're gonna help me."

"Help you what?"

"You recently took a job with D & D Sports, and I'm gonna bring them down."

"What's your problem?"

"They break the law over and over, protecting their so-called *clients*."

"Look, I'm just an employee—"

"You treating patients again, Joe? If I remember right, you're not permitted to practice medicine in New York State."

"I'm an advisor for the company. I just advise."

53

SUSPECT BEHAVIOR

"Uh-huh, I tell you what. You went to jail twice, once for having a massive amount of cocaine, and once for beating a man half to death. I read your file. You beat that man because he was abusing your sister. I know you're not a bad guy. These people, Damon and Dante, are not good people. They've covered up rapes, Joe. I know that doesn't sit well with you. You have two strikes, one more and you get twenty years. Is that what you want?"

"What do you want from me?"

"Help me. If you help me bring them down, I'll make sure you get immunity. I've seen your little girls, Joe. I know you don't want them going up to the state prison to see you for the next twenty years."

"I can't help you, Reyes. I just started working there. They seem on the up and up to me."

"Okay, Joe, okay. I'm gonna leave my card for you. If you change your mind and decide to do the right thing, call me. Have a good night."

"Yeah, yeah sure, you too."

***

It's two am and Dre, the official talker for D & D, is in the bed sleeping hard. After a long day, he came in, worn out. He has his position because he has a gift, the ability to talk persuasively to escape almost any situation. His phone begins to ring. For a second, he considers not answering, but he knows that's not an option.

"Yeah?"

"Dre, it's Damon. Sorry, bro…I know it's late, but I had to call. We got a little job for you."

"Okay bro, what's up?"

"I got a call from Derrick Fair. He was leaving the club and he was drunk. He tried to get home on his own. All I know is there's only one route he could take home and he didn't get there."

"Damn, I'm on my way."

Within moments, Dre is dressed and out the door, speeding toward the route that Derrick would have taken. It's dark and there's no sign of him. The moon is full, and there's not a sound out on the road. After about ten minutes, Dre tries the superstar running back's cell phone, but gets no answer. Finally, he sees the red Ferrari swerving ahead of him. Dre takes a sigh of relief but then quickly realizes it was premature. Before he can reach the car, it swerves into the oncoming lane, causing another car to hit him. Neither one was going that fast, but it was enough to damage both cars. Dre jumps out of his car and runs up, surveying the damage. He knows he has to work fast. He glances into the Ferrari and sees that Derrick is fine, just severely drunk.

"Don't move, man!" Dre tells him, while running over to look at the other car.

He opens the door to the Ford Taurus and finds a young black woman, with a bump on her forehead.

"Are you okay?"

"I-I think so. Can you call 911 for me?" she asks.

"Um…sure, but before I do, did you see the car that hit you?"

"No."

"Take a look."

She struggles with her seatbelt to take a look out her window. She sees the damaged Ferrari and perks up. Even though it's dark out, she tries to make out who the driver is.

"Who is that?" she asks.

"If I tell you that, it would change some things," Dre tells her.

"What do you mean?"

"Do you like football?"

"Yes."

"Cool, who's your team?"

"Philly."

"Well, all I can tell you is that the man in that car plays for Philly. You got a good team this year. What's your name?"

"Tina."

"Tina, if the man in that car gets caught up in a DUI, he could get kicked off the team...your team. I know you don't want that."

"I'm so confused, though. Why won't you tell me who he is? Who are you? I'm gonna need to get looked at."

"Tina, what do you do for a living?"

"I-I'm a student at NYU. I was just driving back from my boyfriend's house."

"A student, huh? Nice. Listen, this car is a 2005 Ford Taurus. It's worth about eight hundred bucks. What if I gave you eight thousand right now?"

"Dollars?"

"Yes, Tina, dollars. You gotta think fast though. We don't have a lot of time."

"I-I can't know who that is?"

"Nope." He quickly grabs a stack of hundreds from his car and begins counting them in front of her.

"Okay, I'll take the money."

"I thought you might," Dre smiles.

"Here you go. Get that cut on your forehead looked at. One more thing, don't ever tell anyone about this."

"Ok, I won't, I promise."

"Good. Take care of yourself, Tina."

She smiles and pulls off.

Quashon Davis

Dre runs over to Derrick's car. He quickly moves him over to the passenger side. He gets in and starts it up.

"Dre? Is that you? Let's get some muffins, bro. I was thinkin' about muffins yesterday and I just want one, bro."

"Shut up and go to sleep."

"I'm not sleepy, man. Is that fajita spot still open? What time is it?"

"Stop talking, D. Fair. Just close your eyes and think about food or something."

"Okay."

As they pull off, Dre quickly calls Damon and tells him to send someone to pick up his car.

"I gotchu, Dre. Good job," says Damon.

"Listen, man, I know D. Fair is a client and your boy, but he's got a real drinking problem, man. This is the fifth time we had to save him from a DUI. I think we should take a hard look at his file tomorrow, bro."

"What do you mean? We're not terminating our contract with him. He's been a client since the beginning."

"I know that. I'm talking about getting him some help. Maybe we could quietly enroll him in rehab or something. I like him too, bro, he's a great guy. But tonight, he hit a young girl, man. He coulda killed her. I just don't want anything bad to happen."

"I get it, Dre. You make a good point. I'll talk to Dante in the morning about it."

"Cool. One more thing, have R.J. look up a Tina driving a blue Ford Taurus, license plate RDS-151."

"Done."

***

The Little Peoples School of The Arts is the premiere kindergarten through twelfth grade institution for kids that have talent. Most kids who attend this school end up professionally singing or dancing. For four-year-old, James Jones, he's already firmly on that path. He plays the piano almost flawlessly and has a golden voice. His dad, Jay, tries to keep the attention off of him, especially after the scandalous way he took him initially. At this school, he can blend in with other talented kids that are above the curve talent-wise.

Tuition is a modest ninety-three grand at TLPSA, and the wealthy have no problem paying it. Some kids as young as two years old, get scholarships to attend. The school is the size of a major college campus, complete with a football field, separate gym for the basketball team, library, cafeteria with several different options, and a skate park. The grounds are always freshly manicured, thanks to Ted Roundtree, the head groundskeeper. He has been keeping everything perfect on campus since 1980. Even though he works at the school of future stars, and interacts with lots of rich parents all the time, Ted doesn't have and doesn't make much money. He loves his job though, and the Christmas cards he gets from parents usually equal his yearly salary. A happy soul, Ted's always singing and always smiling. Every student, parent, and teacher knows and loves Ted. He speaks to everyone, and treats them all like he's known them his whole life. Students love when he tells his old stories, and parents appreciate their kids being influenced by such a jolly old soul.

It's Wednesday, the day he does his grocery shopping, and Ted is slowly going up and down the store aisles, singing Al Green very low. He's in his usual happy mood, and is excited because Wednesdays are half-off soup day. As he loads his cart, he can't help but sing, "Let's Stay Together" just a bit louder.

Suddenly, someone comes from behind him and joins in, flawlessly hitting the notes in the next verse.

Ted turns around and smiles at the beautiful woman that reminds him of his own daughter. They hold the soup cans like microphones and finish the chorus strong, together.

Quashon Davis

"You have a lovely voice, young lady," says Ted.

"Why, thank you, so do you," she replies.

"You have a nice night," he tells her.

She smiles and continues on.

Ted takes his time getting all his groceries together and double-bagging them all, so he doesn't have any problems on the bus. He didn't bring his mini-cart today, so he has to carry them all by hand. As he finishes paying for everything, the store manager tells him to be good on his way out.

Ted begins to walk down the street to the bus stop, when he hears a woman call out to him.

"Hi there, sweet voice. You headed for the bus?"

Ted looks over to see the young woman he shared a brief duet with in the store. She's sitting in a really nice car, smiling at him.

"Hi there, young lady. I hope you keep singing. You have a great voice."

"You catching the bus?"

"Yes, ma'am. The only thing I drive is a lawnmower."

"Those bags look heavy. How would you like a ride?"

"Why would you give an old man like me a ride home? I'm twice your age and I don't have any money."

"Maybe, I'm just nice."

"Well, these old bones could use a ride home, instead of carrying bags on and off the bus."

"So, get in. I'll take you home," she smiles.

He reluctantly puts his bags in the back and gets in her car.

"I'm Ted," he smiles.

"Call me Sapphire," she says.

59

CHAPTER FIVE
GHOSTED WITH ALL BASES COVERED

DRE IS SITTING AT GRAY'S Papaya, one of his favorite places, enjoying a hot dog. He has his laptop open and he's streaming music, tweeting, playing an online game, buying stuff on Amazon, and eating. He's a busy guy without a lot of downtime, so he does a lot of multitasking. He has one earbud in his ear, and has even taken a few phone calls while doing everything else. As he picks up his second hot dog, a call comes through.

"Yeah," he says.

"Hey, it's Dante. We got a major problem, bro."

"What's up?"

Just as Dante begins explaining, he cuts him off. Dre tells him he has to call him back. Standing in front of him is Officer Reyes.

"Andre Daniels, how are you?"

"I'm good. How did you know where I was?"

"You tweeted it fifteen minutes ago. I follow you and all your teammates."

"What do you want, Reyes? Do you ever give up?"

"No, I don't. How's the hot dogs here?"

Quashon Davis

"They're awesome. You want me to order you one?"

"Maybe next time. I'm on the clock."

"If you're on the clock, what are you doing here?"

"Do you know a young woman by the name of Tina Powell?"

"No, should I?"

"Well, maybe. See, a young lady named Tina Powell checked herself into the hospital with a nasty bump on her head. She thought it was nothing, turned out she had major damage. She actually died this morning. We checked her place, and guess what? She had about eight grand in cash."

Even though Dre is nervous and upset, he keeps his cool.

"Okay, so?"

"The cash had your fingerprints on it. That made me think a little. I know you're scum like the rest of D & D, so I went and checked her car. You know what I found? Front-end damage. This is what happened. One of your clients was probably drunk and hit her. You're 'the talker,' so you probably paid her to keep quiet. Well, she's keeping real quiet, Andre, forever."

"I don't know any Tina Powell," says Dre.

"That's what you're sticking to, huh? Listen, you know D & D is going down behind this one. Don't go down with them. If you tell me what you know, I'll keep you out of jail. You have my word."

"I don't know her, Reyes. I drop cash everywhere. Who knows how she got it."

"Oh, come on, Andre. It's over. You know it."

"What do you have? Some cash with my prints on it? Please. If you had something, I'd be in cuffs. I know the law. I feel bad that a young girl lost her life, but I didn't have anything to do with it."

"Okay, fine. If you change your mind, you know how to find me."

Before Reyes is out of sight completely, Dre is already on the phone with Dante.

"The girl is really dead?" he asks.

"Yeah, man. When she hit her head, a blood vessel burst and she didn't know."

"Dante, I-I don't know what to do."

"I got it covered, man. That night when we took your car from the scene, we swept away every print. We picked up every piece of both cars that was left on the ground. As for the cash, don't even worry. I got it covered."

"How?"

"Dre, do you trust me or not, bro? This is what we do."

"Okay, cool."

***

At Diamond Fitness near City Hall, elected official, Don Markos, is running off his taco lunch on the treadmill. The six foot five, Greek man has been in America since the age of eight. He's a young guy with a lot of ideas that aspires to unseat the governor one day. He has a large following of both young and old people, so that day may be sooner, rather than later.

Markos has the same issue that most young guys have. He can't keep anything to himself. He always has to tell everything. The shared generation of young people thinks the word secret is derived from an old deodorant. As he jogs on the treadmill, he tweets to all of his followers, telling them where he is and what he's doing.

"Markos, working hard, I see. You're always here," says a short blonde woman.

"Ah, Natalie, how are you, my dear? They say no pain, no gain."

"I'm okay. I had meetings all day. I was gonna skip my resistance class tonight, but I needed it."

"I understand. I came straight from the office. If I didn't, I would've been home relaxing in my bed watching television."

"That sounds nice. You've never invited me over to watch television."

"My dear Natalie, you know I have a wife at home. Why do you tempt me with your beauty?"

"I'm hoping one day, you'll give in. See you around, Markos."

"Goodnight, my dear."

As Natalie puts a lot of extra switch in her walk, the man on the treadmill next to Markos can't help but take notice.

"She really wants your attention."

"She does. Imagine if she knew you had it, Bengie."

"Poor girl, maybe I'll share with her the secret of holding your interest."

"I don't think she has what it takes," laughs Markos.

"You ready to get outta here?"

"I am."

Once they leave the gym, the two head for Bengie's house. Benjamin Graham is a journalist for the *New York Times*. He's a young guy that's on the fast track to being at the top of the business. Last year, he broke the story of the lieutenant governor taking payments from the mob, and it vaulted him to the top of his business. He has big dreams, but to this point, he hasn't stepped on anyone's toes to achieve them. His affair with Markos would be a big story, but it would most likely derail his career if it came out.

"Bengie, I only have about an hour. I gotta get home," says Markos.

"Hey, you'll make it. We'll get to my place in no time."

"Okay."

"You okay? What's going on?"

"Bengie, I just feel like someone's watching me lately. Ever since Tony was killed, something feels off."

"Tony Alves? You weren't friends with the guy. He was just your drug supplier. He supplied a lot of people with drugs."

"We spoke a lot though. He has a sister in prison that he was trying to get freed. She shouldn't be in there, honestly. They picked her up for a battery charge and kept her. I was trying to help him with it."

"Markos, that's nothing. What are you not telling me?"

"He had this computer drive he was selling. He said it was gonna be his big payday. He stole it from some highly secured office he was supposed to be cleaning. I told him to put it back. When he told me what was on it, I knew right then that it was gonna be bad. I tried to distance myself from him."

"What the hell was on it?" asks Bengie.

"Some bad stuff."

***

Officer Reyes walks into the precinct with a big smile on his face. He thinks this time he's going to nail D & D Sports Management to the wall. When he found the eight thousand at the young girl's house, every single hundred-dollar-bill had Dre's fingerprints on them. He knows something happened that they must've "fixed." He's confident he has them. That much money is enough to get a warrant. He hums a happy tune while he's typing up the warrant for Dre's arrest. Pete walks by and can't help but notice Reyes' good mood. When he asks him what's going on, Reyes happily tells him he's about to pick up one of D & D's employees. Pete tells him he may want to look in interrogation room five before he finishes. Confused,

Quashon Davis

Reyes walks over to see Damon, Dante, Dre and their lawyer, Sue, sitting in the room with Marie. He rushes inside, pissed.

"What the hell is going on here?" he asks.

"We came down to clear the air on this awful Tina Powell situation," Sue says.

"Clear the air? I was on my way to arrest your man here. The girl had eight thousand dollars in her possession and every single bill had his fingerprints on them," laughs Reyes.

Dre starts to say something, but Sue cuts him off.

"Actually, my client can explain that. I suppose you didn't check where the young lady worked?"

"I know how to do my job. She was a waitress at Dave and Busters."

"Yes, she was, during the day. At night, she was a dancer at Obsessions down on Columbus."

"What? Get outta here with that."

Before Reyes can finish, Sue drops a folder on the table.

"There you have pictures of her stripping at Obsessions. Also, there's signed affidavits from the owner, security manager, and two patrons that saw Dre tipping Tina several hundred-dollar bills throughout the course of that night. There's also one signed by Jennifer Gallow, one of the dancers that went home with Dre that night, and says they went straight to his home and she stayed until the next day."

As Reyes goes through everything in the folder, his head looks like it's going to explode. He's changing colors, and clearly getting very angry. Dre, Dante, and Damon are doing all they can to keep from laughing out loud.

"Get the hell out of this precinct," he yells.

"Um, thanks for coming in and sharing this information," Marie says, while looking at Reyes with a confused face.

"I'm tired of these lying bastards getting away with everything. They killed that girl," Reyes blasts after they leave.

"What are you talking about?" Marie asks.

"They did this. I don't know how or why, but they paid that girl off for something that happened that night. She was in an accident. I know it was with one of their clients."

"Should be easy enough to figure out. What color paint was on her car?"

"Red."

"Okay, so look up their client list. It's public knowledge. Filter out the ones that have red cars, then take out the ones that have had DUI's in the past. I'll bet you find your guy."

Reyes is at a computer less than ten seconds before Marie stops talking. He looks up the information and a big smile comes across his face. Moments later, his squad car is speeding toward Derrick Fair's home. He convinced Marie to take the ride with him.

"Are you okay?" she asks.

"I will be when we get there and find his car."

"You don't have a warrant, Reyes."

"We're just gonna ask him if we can look around. If he says yes, we're good."

"You really do want these guys bad."

"These people, they call themselves a sports agency, but they're pure evil. They break any and every law to get their clients out of trouble. Every time I get close to catching these bastards, they find a way to cover up their crap. They're always a step ahead. They smile in my face, knowing that I know how dirty they are. They mock me, because they know I can never pin anything on them."

"Did these guys sleep with your lady or something? That's a lot."

"No, I'm just tired of watching them get away with it. It's time to bring them down once and for all."

"Damn Reyes, okay. Change the subject."

Quashon Davis

"Fine, Marie. How do you feel with Roger being back? I know that was a big surprise."

"Yeah, it was. When he fled the country, I didn't think he would ever come back."

"How do you end up sleeping with your partner's wife?"

"It just happened."

"Come on. That doesn't just happen. Everyone loved Roger, except the captain. People must've looked at you like you were a monster."

"They still do. It doesn't bother me though."

"Why?"

"Me and Miesha were made for each other. It wasn't a personal thing against Roger. It is what it is. Sure, a lotta cops looked at me afterwards like I was a bitch for doing that to him. You know the funny thing? I am a bitch. I never pretend to be anything different. It's a man's world. I'm a woman that takes what she wants in this man's world. You know what, I wanted his wife. I won't apologize for it. I got plenty of evil looks from cops after everything went down with Raj, but no one had the stones to say anything to me. If the result of hurting one of my friends is me getting years of pleasure, I'll hurt my friend every time. Yeah, he would tell me about it when they were having problems. And sure, I used that information to my advantage. Would I change anything if I could? Nope. And, anyone that has a problem with that can come see these hands."

"Uh…okay. You look like you have a black eye right now. Maybe you should tone it down a little."

"I don't need to tone anything down. I had to be twice as tough to make the force. Rayton treats me like a child. I'm tougher than half those guys in that precinct."

"I'm glad we're here," says Reyes.

SUSPECT BEHAVIOR

As they get out of the car and head to the massive gate, there's Derrick Fair, washing all eight of his cars. He's careful and meticulous, washing each one individually. He sees Marie and Reyes and gives them a welcoming smile, while inviting them in. They question him about the other night, but Derrick was so drunk he doesn't remember anything. An honest guy, Derrick is upfront about being too drunk to remember anything from that night. Reyes knows he's got it though. In the corner, he sees the red Ferrari. A smile comes across his face from ear to ear. He tells Marie to arrest Derrick while he walks over to it. Instead of her following his instructions, she just stares at him confused. Reyes walks up and his smile is wiped quickly from his face. The Ferrari is in pristine shape. There's not a scratch on it. He walks all around the car before looking underneath it. He opens the trunk, checks the glove compartment, and finds nothing.

"How did they do this?" Reyes yells at Derrick.

"How did who do what?"

"How did D & D fix your car that fast? How?"

"What's wrong with you, man? I don't know what you're talkin' about."

"Let's go, Reyes," Marie says, pulling him by his shirt.

He angrily gets in his car and speeds off toward the expressway.

***

Across town in a small garage are Dante and Dre. They are standing with Ray, their private mechanic they have on their payroll. The three of them are standing in front of Derrick's Ferrari that has major front-end damage.

"How long, Ray?"

"Eh, gimme two weeks. I'll knock it out," he responds.

"I'll give you one week," Dante says, placing a large amount of cash on his toolbox.

Quashon Davis

"A week it is. You're the boss."

"You know Reyes is gonna figure out it was Derrick," says Dre.

"Yeah, maybe. If he does, I left my Ferrari at Derrick's house, just switched the plates."

"Smart, but what about the VIN number?"

"Reyes ain't that smart, Dre. Know your personnel. He goes on emotions, that's why he's not a real threat."

"But, Derrick is an honest guy."

"He doesn't even know we switched his car out. He may be a drunk, but he's a good guy. I wouldn't take the chance. When Ray finishes fixing it, I'll switch it out again without him knowing it. Don't worry so much, Dre. I'm always on top of everything."

***

Markos leaves Bengie's apartment and heads for his car. He only had an hour to spare and ended up staying for two. His wife called him twice already, and his mind is just waking up. He quickly begins formulating what he's going to say. Before he gets in the car, he quickly dials Bengie first.

"Hey, what's up? You forgot something?"

"I think I left my watch on your dresser," says Markos.

"I'll bring it out."

"No, don't worry about it. Listen, I shouldn't have told you about that drive. Don't tell anyone. You can't write a story on it. You know that."

"I'm not stupid, Markos. I know better. I've kept us a secret this long; I think I know how to keep my mouth shut. Besides, you wouldn't even tell me what's on it."

"That's for your safety. I guess I'm just a little nervous. I mean, Tony was killed, you know."

69

"Tony was into drugs. He dealt with shady characters. That's what got him killed."

"Bengie, what if whatever was on that drive got him killed?"

"I think it was who he was that got him killed, Markos, but anything is possible. If important people feel threatened, you never know."

"Exactly. You see my point. We can't be sure."

"Even if you're right, Tony was a drug-dealing crook that came across the drive. No one's gonna think twice about him being gone. You're an elected official. People would miss you, they'd notice. Trust me. You got nothing to worry about."

"When something threatens powerful people, there's plenty to worry about. This isn't some little money scheme that cheated a few people out of a few bucks. Folks could get dragged outta some high-profile places behind this."

"What are you gonna do?"

"I'm not gonna do anything. I'm gonna act like I never saw it. I'm gonna go on with my life, eventually be the mayor, then the governor. I'm not looking back."

"But, if it's as big as you say, if it ever gets out and people find out you knew about it, you'd be finished too."

"I just need some time to think, Bengie. I'll figure it out."

"You know I'm here if you need me."

"I know, I'll talk to you soon."

"Okay."

Markos decides to call his wife later. He grabs the door handle to his car and feels a surge of heat course through his body. In a second, a rush of diarrhea fills his bowels and a load of vomit fills his mouth. Before he can process what's happening, he falls over, unconscious. The block is full of people who either scream or run towards him. Markos is frothing at the mouth, barely breathing.

Quashon Davis

***

Roger sits in his temporary office, typing on his computer. It's like old times for him, as he tries to track down The Ghost while he has a ton of other things on his mind. He knows he has to be focused completely on The Ghost or he'll fail. Unfortunately for him, being out of the country for four years has left him with a ton of things to catch up with. While he quietly checks out his ex-wife's social media page, he's making a list of things to see and do.

"I can't believe the *Black Panther* finally got a movie," he says to himself.

While doing all these non-work related things, he has managed to search for clues regarding The Ghost. Unfortunately, he's hit a wall. Seven years ago, when he almost caught her, he was at the right place at the right time. She had just assassinated a wealthy businessman by shooting him from about a hundred yards away. While everyone was screaming and running, Roger was surveying the area. He noticed one woman among the hundreds at the scene that wasn't running. Her face was partially covered, and she was casually walking away. He ran after her and even managed to grab her, before she stabbed him in the ribs with a small knife and got away.

He's reminiscing over that, scouring the internet for clues, and looking at all the pictures on Miesha's Facebook page. Surprisingly, there are no pictures or talk of his partner, Marie, at all. There's nothing to suggest they live together or anything. In the four years since he's been gone, Miesha's only put a handful of new pictures of herself on her page. He uses his anger toward what happened to mask the fact that he misses her and their marriage. He's wanted to reach out to her since he got back, but the betrayal he feels is keeping him from doing it. The embarrassment and disrespect he felt when everything came out, still hurts him. His feelings for his first and only love are still there though. She's still programmed in his phone.

71

Could she still have the same number? Does she still think about him the way he thinks about her? Does she feel bad about it? Is she happy? He stares at his phone for a long time. He slowly scrolls to her name and takes a long time, thinking about what to do next. As his finger reaches for the call button, a call comes through.

"This is Roger."

"Hey, Raj, it's Pete."

"Hey. What's up?"

"I just got a call that an elected official died on the street uptown. They're saying it could be murder. I was told to tell you."

"I'm on my way. What are you doing right now, Pete?"

"Eating a sandwich."

"Take the ride with me. Meet me out front."

"Like old times!"

***

The two head for the crime scene and Roger fills Pete in on The Ghost. Roger was Pete's first partner and he has a great deal of respect for him. Even though they had a falling out of sorts that caused Pete to request a new partner, and Roger shot him years later, thinking he was messing with Miesha, they still remain cool enough to work together and talk. Pete is *Captain America* before the experiment. He's a five foot seven, frail, white guy that's been beaten up by several suspects over the years. He has no fear though, and that's why Roger respects him. He wasn't happy about what happened, but he understood the emotions Roger must've felt at the time. There was a lot, however, that he didn't understand. Even though they were having a fallout at the time, Pete never understood how Roger could think he would betray him like that.

"Raj, you shot me in front of your house and left me laying in the street. I forgave you. You knew Miesha was cheating on you and I know you were full of emotions. You saw me coming out of your house and you reacted. I went to your house to warn you about what was going on. I know you shot me in the vest on purpose. I never took it personal. What I didn't understand was how you thought I was capable of sneaking around with your wife. I never would've done that. I thought of you and Esh as family. Our views were different when Jay got in trouble, so I didn't want to be partners anymore. It didn't change anything as far as I was concerned. It was the job. You never even checked on me, man."

"I'm a damn good detective, Pete, one of the best. My wife was cheating on me and I couldn't figure out why or with who. I followed clues, asked her, and I was stuck. I never get stuck, Pete. The only woman I ever cared about was sneaking around behind my back with someone else. The worst part was it was my fault. I let the job become more important than her. She kept asking me to stay home more, give her more time, do more things with her. I wouldn't listen. I was cracking high-profile cases and my name was always in the papers. I loved it. Before I knew it I was working seven days a week, leaving Esh in the house alone. The mayor gave me the key to the city. The little bit of time I was home every week, everything felt normal. I thought I had everything.

"One day, I figured out she was cheating on me and I cracked. I couldn't think straight. I was drinking a lot, and instead of trying to fix my marriage, I was concentrated on finding out who she was seeing. I came home one day and saw you hugging Esh and I snapped. I just wanted to hurt you. I knew you had your vest on, so I put a couple of bullets in it. I was wrong though, really wrong. I didn't realize it was my partner, Marie, until it was too late. She sat in that squad car week after week, listening to me talk about my marriage. The whole time, she was tearing it apart. You didn't agree with how I handled the Jay situation, and even though I didn't like it, I understood. You requested a new partner, but you never sold me out. I apologize, man. I really wish that mess never happened," Roger admits.

"I appreciate that. Now, let's move on from all this mushy stuff. We're good."

***

They arrive at the crime scene. There are people everywhere, including news reporters, and bright yellow tape separating all of them from the body of Don Markos. He's crumpled up, laying in the fetal position on the ground by his car door. They make their way over to him, briefly greeting the other officers on the way. Markos is on his side with foam coming from his mouth. His cell phone is lying next to him, showing several missed calls and texts. Roger and Pete glance at each other, before taking out their disposable gloves and putting them on.

"How do you know The Ghost is responsible for this?" Pete asks.

"I just know."

"I'm guessing he was poisoned."

"Yeah, Pete. What gave it away? Him looking like a dog with rabies?"

"Still a smart ass, I see."

"Pete, look at his hand. It's red and full of burns and blisters. Don't touch it, and don't touch the car."

"Why? We got gloves on."

"Whatever poisoned him was powerful enough to put him down before he got in his car. Judging by his hand, it might've been on the door handle. Get one of these guys to check it out. Hey, Officer! Tell me what you guys know so far."

"Yes, sir. Deputy Governor, Don Markos. We don't know why he was here. He lives about thirty minutes away. CSI says it looks like it was a fast-moving neurotoxin, but they didn't touch anything until you got here."

Quashon Davis

"Good. Dump his phone and tell me the last number he called."

"Right away, Detective."

Roger takes out his tiny flashlight and begins inspecting the car door handle. He takes his time, examining every inch. He finds fresh fingerprints, proving that Markos touched the door handle. He knows it must've been The Ghost. This assassination was too sophisticated. What he can't figure out is why this low-level official was the victim of it. Ever since he got back, he's been two steps behind The Ghost, and he doesn't like it. The distractions that go along with returning after four years away are overwhelming.

"Pete, this neurotoxin may be the most powerful poison I've ever seen," he says.

"Me too. But, how many people would have access to this?"

"That I don't know. This is some professional stuff, man. Hits aren't supposed to be this clean. The Ghost is worth every penny."

"Raj, you sound like you admire The Ghost."

"I don't. I admire the work ethic."

"Detectives, the last call the victim made was to a man named Benjamin Graham. He's a journalist for the *Times*," says a junior officer.

"Thank you for that. You got an address for him? Pete, we're gonna hafta head there."

"Actually, he lives right there," the officer says, pointing a few houses down.

Roger and Pete glance at each other before getting up from the crime scene and heading to the home of Benjamin Graham. They head up the porch stairs, both pulling their guns. This is the last man to see Markos alive. He could have had something to do with his death. They knock on the door and take a step back. The door opens slowly and there's Bengie, shaking with his face engulfed in tears. He lets them both enter his home.

"I didn't kill Markos, I love him. He was here with me for about an hour. He was about to go home to his family. I heard people screaming outside and looked out the window. M-Markos was on the ground. I knew he was dead. You see, he had a bad addiction to heroin. I tried to get him to stop, but he was too hooked on it. His guy…supplier…whatever, was a guy named Tony Alves. Tony was a dirt bag, and at night he cleaned government offices for a living. He got his hands on a drive that had something on it and some important people didn't want it to ever get out. H-He wouldn't tell me what it was, but he said he was in danger."

Roger can tell that Bengie is telling the truth. The Ghost has claimed another victim, and he's no closer to catching the killer. Eventually, the FBI is going to start questioning their choice to clear him and bring him in. It's time to focus and get ahead of The Ghost.

I know exactly what to do, he thinks.

CHAPTER SIX
A SUSPECT OR A DESPERATE REACH?

THAT EVENING, ROGER CATCHES UP with Jay and they decide to get dinner. Doing anything with Jay is tough. He can only go places that cost a lot of money. He doesn't do this because he wants to. Instead, he does it because he has to. With his level of popularity, going to normal places can be cataclysmic. He's mobbed most places he goes, so he's always wearing a disguise, a big hoodie, or a hat and shades. The cost of being one of the best basketball players that's ever lived is great, but Jay doesn't mind paying it. Roger was planning on sitting in his hotel room all night examining evidence, going over the particulars of the case, but Jay convinced him to come out for a little while.

They decide to go to R & B's, one of their favorite spots over the years. It's a restaurant that always has live music being performed. Once a breeding ground for up and coming famous singers, it has begun to experience a slight decline. It's always packed, but the talent level isn't what it used to be. It started as a hole in the wall and over time, grew into one of the hottest spots in the city. The owner, Irene "Ma" Turner eventually was able to buy the property next door and expand R & B's. Their food more than makes up for the recent lack of talent on stage. They have the best soul food in the city.

SUSPECT BEHAVIOR

Jay and Roger pull up in front of R & B's. There's a line outside of people waiting to get in, as is always the case. Everyone is struggling, trying to see through the tinted windows in Jay's Mercedes. The car sits quietly until an attendant comes up. He opens the passenger door and Roger steps out. The crowd continues chattering until he goes over to the driver's side door and Jay gets out. Everyone loses their minds. There's cheering and yelling coming from everywhere. Jay waves and smiles as he and Roger quickly head inside. Security whisks them by everyone to a private table in the back that's roped off. Two security guards stand in front of the ropes. Everyone is staring and carrying on.

"You just had to come here, didn't you?" asks Roger.

"You love this place, man."

Ma Turner comes out of the kitchen to hug and kiss Roger and Jay. She's known them since they were kids playing in the neighborhood.

"My boys, it's so good to see you both. Still friends after all these years. I love it. When you two are ready to order, you tell one of these guys to come and get me. You understand?"

"You don't hafta do that, Ma," says Jay.

"You heard what I said, right?"

"Yes, Ma," they both say with a smile.

Ma Turner walks off with a little pep in her step. Jay in the building means people texting and tweeting, and more business coming.

"See, Raj, Ma Turner missed us. You know you're glad we came," says Jay.

"Do you see how everybody's carrying on? If these two guards weren't here, those women would jump you like a *Walking Dead* scene."

"Probably, but we're about to have Ma's mac and cheese."

"Amen to that."

Quashon Davis

"So, what's going on? You get any closer to catching The Ghost?"

"Naw, bro. She doesn't make mistakes, doesn't leave clues. It's not like some terrorist crap, she won't kill a bus or train load of people to get one person. She just gets her target. It's always neat and clean."

"Raj, you sound like you admire this psycho."

"Naw, I don't. I respect the work ethic though."

"Huh?"

"The Ghost is like the Kobe Bryant of assassins."

"Oh, I actually think I understood that."

"I'm getting closer, though."

"Does she operate in other countries?" asks Jay.

"Of course. Whoever's paying. Last year, she killed a diplomat in Pamplona. The Ghost is good, but she never stays in one place that long. Whatever's got her here must be big. The window to catch her is closing fast, though."

"Well, you're off the clock now. All you gotta worry about is whether you're gettin' collards or string beans."

"I hear that."

A steady stream of men and women come up to the table to get a picture of Jay. Despite the two guards, he's friendly to everyone. He even comes down and takes pictures with people. Roger watches Jay pose with person after person, taking picture after picture. He can't understand how he does it. While he drinks his water, getting a kick out of watching, he sees a familiar face off in the distance. Sitting at a table is his new friend, Maya. Roger stands up to make sure it's her. Sure enough, there's Maya, sitting at a table with her friends.

"Excuse me, superstar, you mind if I invite my new lady friend and her people to eat with us?" Roger asks,

"New lady friend? Really? You're just mentioning this now? That's fine with me, Raj. Just be ready for a major Q &

79

A session when we get to the car later," Jay says, while posing for pictures. Roger makes his way past him and walks over to Maya's table. Her friends look up in amazement at the six-eight giant. They're all smiles, except Maya. She has the same blank expression on her face that she always does.

"Roger, what a surprise. It's good to see you," she says.

"Yes, I can tell by your face that you're happy to see me."

The other women giggle as Maya continues with her stoic gaze.

"What are you doing here, Roger?"

"I'm here having dinner with one of my boys. Actually, it's Jay. Jay Jones, used to play for the Knicks. Would you and your friends like to join us?"

"I appreciate that Roger, but we..."

Angie, Cian, and Tess almost knock Maya to the floor in order to get up from the table and head over to the VIP area with Roger. Maya reluctantly brings up the rear. He introduces them all to Jay, who is still greeting people and taking pictures. The women all sit down with Roger, while Jay wraps up.

"I don't think Maya mentioned you," says Tess.

"She didn't. We would've remembered," Cian agrees.

"I met Roger at my gym. We just went to dinner once. Anyway, this is Angie, Cian, and Tess."

"Ladies, it's a pleasure."

"You tall. What size shoe you wear?" asks Angie.

"I wear a seventeen," he says

"Damn. You gonna be walkin' like a ballerina, girl," laughs Angie.

"Can you *please* not be you today?" Maya asks.

Jay sits down and everyone introduces themselves. They order their food and drinks and Ma Turner races off, excited to make it happen.

Quashon Davis

"So, Jay, I know you're married, but do you mess around?" asks Angie.

"Oh God..." mumbles Tess.

"Uh, no, I don't."

"Really? How do you do that with all that money? You can have any woman you want."

"I already have her," he says.

"Awwwww..." the women all say.

"I'm not buying it. If I offered you some, you would take it," Angie continues.

"So, what do you ladies do?" asks Jay, changing the subject.

"Well, I'm a dentist," Maya says.

"I'm a consultant for the Navy," Angie says.

"I'm a contractor for a defense company," Cian adds.

"I'm a small business owner," says Tess.

"Wow, you ladies are impressive. I like that," says Jay.

"Do you ever get tired of all the attention? I mean, why not live in a mansion on a mountain somewhere, where you never hafta see people? You literally took about a hundred pictures with people in that little bit of time when we first walked over here. You must get tired of people," says Tess.

"I do. I get tired of people a lot. There are days when I don't feel like signing autographs or taking pictures, but I do it. When I was growing up, I played ball down on West 4th Street. Back then, you had to be a real baller to play there. I can remember times when superstars showed up to watch. People would try to talk to them, take pictures, get autographs, and they would say no every time. I would see ball players around town and they would burn anyone that approached them. I swore when I made it big, I would be the opposite of those guys. The same kids that used to watch me in the park know I'm the same guy today. I try to remember names if I can. I encourage people to approach me. I'm a regular guy. I eat a lot of pizza, watch Netflix, and I love a good milkshake."

"That's cool," says Maya.

"I don't want to talk about me, though. How'd you ladies all meet?" he asks.

"Well, we were all in the service. I was in the Army with Tess. Angie was in the Navy, and Cian was a Marine. We met Angie and Cian at the gym right after we all finished serving. We had a lot in common and we've been tight ever since. I saw these girls working out and I knew they were fellow service members."

"That's cool. I've been friends with Raj for over thirty years. Believe me when I tell you, we've seen it all."

"Do tell," Cian urges.

"Oh, I won't put all our business out there. But, we've seen some things."

"I appreciate that," Raj says sarcastically.

Angie says, "So, since were in the super VIP section, are we getting a bottle?"

"Come on, Angie. Why you gotta try to take advantage?" asks Tess.

"Take advantage? This brotha must be worth nine figures! Think about that."

"When you put it that way, that is a lot of figures," Tess agrees.

"I apologize for them," Maya says.

"No need. It's all good. Yes, let's get some bottles over here," Jay says, signaling the waitress.

"Maya told me she was in Iraq more than once. Did the rest of you ever go to war?" asks Raj.

They all nod in agreement. Roger and Jay are stunned by that. As the night goes on, everyone relaxes and just enjoys each other's company. Roger pays close attention to Maya in an effort to see if she's any different around her friends. To his surprise, she's exactly the same. She never smiles, never frowns, and doesn't show any emotion at all. Even when the table erupts with laughter, she sits with the same blank expression on her face. He was pretty sure that when she got some alcohol in her, everything would change. He was wrong. If anything, she's more robotic than before. Jay has told them story after story and the table has been laughing all night, except for Maya. When the bill comes, it's twelve hundred dollars. Jay calmly takes his card out and gives a five-hundred-dollar tip.

"You're so generous," says Cian.

"Not really. I try to give when I can, though."

"Last year, I went to the Running of the Bulls and while I was out there, nobody ever tipped," Cian says.

"That's crazy. I always wanted to do that. I keep saying I'm gonna try it one day."

"You should, Jay, it's amazing. I was coming back from London and I just figured, why not? I always wanted to do it."

"What company do you work for?" asks Roger.

"Global Force. We're one of the top defense companies in the world," Cian replies.

"Ladies, I had a great time. Maya, take care of him, he's delicate," laughs Jay.

"I will, Jay."

Forty-five minutes later…

"Okay, what's up, Raj? You haven't said a word since we left the restaurant. Did I say something wrong while we were there?" Jay asks.

"No, man. You were fine."

"What's the deal, then? That Maya is fine as hell, bro. They all were. Even that crazy Angie, who tried to write her number on the dinner receipt."

"It can't be this easy. There's millions of people in this city. It can't happen this way."

"What can't, Raj? What are you talking about?"

"Cian."

"Okay...Cian what, exactly?"

"I think Cian is The Ghost."

"Raj, you're one of the best detectives in the world. You live in a city with eight and a half million people. You can't think you randomly ran into the person you're searching for among that many people. You're better than that."

"Before these New York killings, do you know the last two places The Ghost struck?"

"No."

"London and Spain."

"She never said when she was in those places. It could've been anytime."

"No. She said she did the Running of the Bulls. That's between the sixth and fourteenth of July. The Ghost killed a diplomat on July ninth in Pamplona, Spain. The other killing was ten days before that, June thirtieth in London."

"Come on, Raj. That's the Grey Goose talkin'. You know you're being ridiculous."

"Global Force Defense makes all types of weapons for every branch of the military. She would have access to every kind of chemical agent. Traveling for the job would keep her on the books, while she's out there eliminating targets."

"Roger, you need a good night's sleep, that's all."

"Jay, thanks for dinner. I'll call you tomorrow."

Quashon Davis

"Raj, wait. You don't hafta stay in that hotel, bro. You know you're welcome to stay at my house. We got plenty of rooms. You wouldn't even hafta see us if you didn't want to. Shel and James would love to see you."

"Just give me a couple of days to pull some all-nighters. I'll need a place while I look for an apartment. I'll take you up on it next week."

"Okay, Raj. Don't do anything crazy. Get a good night's sleep and see how you feel in the morning."

"Okay, bro."

***

Roger gets out of the car and immediately walks over to his car. He logs into the NYPD database and looks up Cian by her job. Once he has her address, he speeds toward her location. In just under twenty minutes, he's taken a ride that should've taken an hour. He pulls across the street from her house and pulls out his binoculars. It's around 1:30 am, and Cian is working out. He watches her intense workout routine that goes on for about an hour. Once she's done, she heads upstairs and into the shower. Roger patiently waits for her to go to bed. When she comes out of the shower, Cian walks around her bedroom nude, drying herself off, then powdering. Roger watches carefully and intensely. Even though Cian's body is a sight to behold, he's looking for a distinguishing mark. As she turns on the television and gets in the bed, he notices a small tattoo on her left thigh. He can't make out what it is, but it doesn't matter. She turns out the lights and goes to sleep. Roger puts his seat back and does the same.

***

Dante lets out a major yawn as he walks into Starbucks to get his morning coffee. The agency has been busy the last few weeks, signing and recruiting young athletes, fixing situations, and making appearances. Their popularity has grown a thousand percent over the last couple of years. In the sports world, athletes love Dante. In the legal world, cops and attorneys hate him. They can never tie D & D to any scandals. He's always a step ahead. With all he has going on, the one thing he looks forward to every day is his morning coffee.

He orders his coffee while he's looking at his phone. He's always checking his stocks. Dante looks like money, well-dressed, from his shoes to his derby-like hat. He gets his coffee and heads for the door. Before he can get to his car, a young woman stops him. She looks distressed, but Dante is always in a hurry.

"I really don't have time today, young lady," he says.

"You're Dante Sproles."

"Yes, I am, and I'm a busy man. What can I do for you?"

"My name is Dez. I-I ummmm, I'm R.J.'s girlfriend."

"Oh, I'm sorry. I didn't know. How are you?"

"I'm okay, but I have something I'm a little concerned about."

"What's up?" he asks.

"When R.J. came home the other day, there was a cop outside. He told him that he was taking you down and R.J. needed to make a choice whether or not he was going down too."

"Is that right?"

"I told him to call you and tell you right away, but he told me to mind my business."

"You did the right thing by coming to me," Dante says.

"I have student loans and I need him to keep this job. One day, we'll be official and he'll take care of them."

"How much do you owe?"

"About seventy-four grand."

"He makes that in three months."

"I know, but we're not an official couple yet. I just make his meals, keep his house clean, give him sex, and listen when he needs to talk."

"I see. Well, there's many jobs available at D & D Sports Management. Some of them don't even require you to show up to the office, or ever punch a clock. Some could be as simple as observe and report."

"What does a job like that pay?" she asks.

"About seventy-four grand," he replies.

***

Roger watches as Cian walks down her porch stairs with a small suitcase and gets in her car. He put a tracker on it around 4:00 am. Once she pulls off, he waits the standard ten minutes, just in case she forgot something. He then makes his way over to her house and quickly picks her lock. Once inside, Roger puts a pair of latex gloves on and begins searching. The home is one of the cleanest he's ever seen. There's no dirt or trash anywhere. He goes through every room searching thoroughly, but there doesn't seem to be anything to find. There's a picture on her mantle of her running with the bulls. She has awards from Spartan and Tough Mudder run competitions. He makes his way to her bedroom and finds another dead end. He does find handcuffs, chains, and whips though. After searching the house for two hours, he's ready to leave. Even though Roger didn't find a shred of evidence, he's still convinced Cian is The Ghost. He gets into his car and pulls up the tracker he placed on her car. It's at the airport. After thinking for a second, he calls Maya.

"Hey, Raj."

"Hey, good morning. How are you?"

"I'm tired, but I'm okay. I'm heading into work. What's up?"

"I was thinking about the great time I had last night."

"I did too. I know my friends are crazy, but they're good people."

"Yeah, they are. Jay and I were talking about going out again tonight or tomorrow. What are you and your friends up to?"

"Well, I'm free, but Tess is gonna be out of town, Cian is heading out of town today, and Angie is on a project the rest of the week."

"Wow, busy people. I get it. Well, maybe you and I can get together and do something then."

"I'd like that."

"Good. Have a good workday and I'll talk to you later."

"Bye, Roger."

He sits silent for a few minutes, trying to think. There are too many thoughts going through his mind. He needs to know Cian got on that plane. As he fights through all the thoughts on his mind, something hits him that he didn't think of— Bengie. If anyone knew Markos was seeing him, there's the possibility he shared what's on that drive with him. That would make Bengie The Ghost's next target.

***

Joe walks up the stairs and knocks on the door, visibly annoyed. He's not in a good mood at all. He's quickly realizing that because of who he is, this may be too difficult for him. He takes a deep breath and tries to relax. The door opens and there's Jack Bixby. The giant offensive lineman looks Joe up and down, then lets him in without saying a word. Joe walks into the living room area where a young woman is sitting on the floor. Her mouth is bleeding and she's crying. The scene angers Joe to the point where he can feel his hands trembling. He walks up to her and examines her injury. When she was hit, she bit through her tongue.

Quashon Davis

"I'm gonna need eighty-five hundred in cash from you," Joe says.

Bixby takes it from a drawer and throws it over toward him.

"Just drop her off at the bus stop down the street when you're done," he says, walking up the stairs to his bedroom.

Joe angrily begins stitching up her tongue. Violence toward women doesn't work for him at all, under any circumstances. He wants to quit, but the money is just too good. He can now afford a place where both of his daughters can have their own room. He can buy them things he couldn't afford before. He doesn't know what to do.

"Don't try to talk. I'll have this stitched up pretty fast. Don't ever talk to this man again. He's dangerous and he's bad news. Do you understand?"

She nods her head in agreement while he continues to work on her.

"This man could've killed you. As bad as this is, it could've been much worse. I'll take you home when I'm done."

***

Dante walks into D & D with his coffee in hand. He gets off the elevator and heads to his office. He runs into Damon, who's sitting at his desk with his feet up. Damon asks him, "Where's my coffee?" After a few minutes of talk, he makes his way to his office and quickly hangs up his coat. He wasn't lying earlier, Dante is a busy man. Within minutes, he's on his computer, typing away.

"What are we gonna do about Reyes, though?" Damon asks, walking into his office.

"Reyes? Nothin'. That guy ain't smart enough to stop us. If I thought he was a threat, I'd be concerned. He's got nothin' on us. We're always a step ahead."

"Cool. Anything going on, besides the usual craziness?"

"Not yet, bro."

"Good morning, fellas," says Dre, walking in.

"Dre. What's good?"

"Are we gonna talk about Derrick Fair?" Dre asks.

"What about him?" asks Dante.

"He killed that girl, man. He killed her. We didn't just do the D & D thing and cover up a DUI or an assault. We covered up a damn manslaughter."

"Hold on, Dre, that's not true. We covered up our client's minor fender bender, and the girl ended up dying much later," Dante says.

"I ride with y'all to the end, bro. I got y'all backs, no matter what. I just feel bad. The girl was nice."

"I get it, Dre. I know what you're thinking too. If we didn't cover up all his DUI's before that one, would the girl still be alive? It's a valid question. Trust me, she wouldn't. It's already written how we're all gonna die, and there's nothin' we can do to change it. It was her time to go, man. If D. Fair wouldn't have done it on that road, the next car would've. Right now, we have a lot of clients. I get why you're feelin' what you're feelin', but we gotta move on."

"Okay, Dante, you're right. I'll be okay."

"Reyes has been all over us lately. He wants us bad. We gotta be on top of our game, twenty-four-seven," says Dante.

"What about D. Fair? Can we get him in some sorta rehab somewhere?" asks Dre.

"Right now, we can't. With Reyes lurking around, it would be like putting a bullseye on him. When the dust settles, we'll quietly put him in one," Dante replies.

"Agreed," says Damon.

"Yeah, that makes sense," Dre admits.

CHAPTER SEVEN
ALMOST GOT HER. . .AGAIN

JAY AND HIS WIFE, SHEL, pull up at TLPSA to pick up their son. He comes running to the car and jumps in. His excitement is overflowing.

"How was school?" asks Shel.

"I met Sapphire," he blasts.

Jay feels a rumble in his stomach and nervous feelings try to overtake him. He does his best to fight through it.

"You did?" he asks.

"Yeah, we sang together and everything!"

"Wow. What was she at your school for, sweetie?" asks Shel.

"She wanted to hear me sing. It was awesome."

"Hmmm, I remember that time she tweeted about having a crush on you, Jay. She better not be trying to use our son to get close to you."

"I'm sure that's not the case. Word is just starting to spread that this little guy has talent. You want some ice cream?"

"Yeah."

Jay drives straight to the ice cream parlor. He figures giving him ice cream might keep him quiet about the rest of this meeting. When they get to the ice cream parlor, he tries to call Roger, but there's no answer.

***

Bengie is waiting for the train to go to work. He thought about taking the day off, but decided not to. As the train pulls in, he's in a daze thinking about Markos. He takes a seat and begins reading the paper. He still can't believe what happened. As if it couldn't get any crazier, he's been tasked with writing the story on Markos' death for the *Times*. If only he had told him what was on that drive. He could've written a story on it and blew this secret out of the water. Hell, everyone is going to think he knows anyway. Tired, sad and miserable, he calls his editor.

"What, Bengie? I'm busy over here."

"I don't want to write the Don Markos story, Chief. I don't have time."

"Is that right? I didn't realize I was inconveniencing you."

"I just don't have the time right now, that's all."

"I see. This wouldn't have anything to do with him dying fifty feet from your doorstep, would it?"

"No, Chief."

"Uh-huh. Fine, I'll get somebody else to write the story, you little prick."

"Thanks, Chief."

"Whatever," he says, hanging up.

In his depressed state, he never looks at the woman sitting next to him, with her face covered by a veil. Within seconds, he feels a needle pierce his neck, then darkness. The woman checks to make sure he's dead before she stands up. Once she does, the inner train door opens and in walks Roger. He looks at her standing by Bengie's corpse, slumped in the train seat.

Quashon Davis

They stare at each other for several seconds. He can't make out her face through the dark veil, so he just stares intently into her eyes.

"It's the end of the line, Ghost. You're coming with me," he says.

She rushes into the next car while Roger gives chase. As he comes through the inside door, two knives hit him square in his stomach. He looks down and sees them lodged in his gut. Passengers are screaming and cowering in fear. Roger thought he planned for everything, but he didn't wear his vest. He goes to take another step and the room starts spinning. Before he realizes what's happening, he's on the ground. Right before he passes out, he sees The Ghost get off the train as it comes to its scheduled stop. She takes off running and he passes out.

***

It's a rainy afternoon at Forest Hills Cemetery and everyone is standing around with dark umbrellas. The mood is somber. The preacher just finished giving the eulogy. Tina Powell's parents are too shaken up to speak. They are sitting in front of their daughter's casket, stone-faced. They're both still in shock, and still don't know what happened. Her friends are all in tears, as are her other family members. As the casket is being lowered into the ground, you can hear crying coming from every direction. It's the scenario every parent fears the most, burying your own child. The mother breaks down and begins crying hysterically, while the dad just stares off into space. The service is officially over, but no one is leaving. Everyone is just standing around talking, some patting the dad on the back, or lightly rubbing the mom's shoulders. She was their only child.

About a hundred yards away from the people, Dre stands watching. He has tears in his eyes and binoculars in his hands. He feels terrible about what happened. He hasn't slept in days, and he's even felt ill. Through the binoculars, he sees the hurt in the parents' faces, and it makes him feel even worse. As much as Dre loves his job, loves his bosses, loves what he does, this whole situation just feels wrong to him. A young girl is dead and he helped cover it up, because one of the company's clients did it. It's not sitting well with him.

"Why so far away from the action?" a voice asks from over his right shoulder.

Dre turns around to see a beautiful woman. She's tall, curvaceous and doing things to her fitted black dress.

"Oh, I uh...I didn't want to really be seen," he says.

"I understand. How did you know my cousin?" she asks.

There's a long hesitation on Dre's part. "I, um...well she...I-I didn't actually know her. I uh...used to work with her."

"Oh, okay. You don't hafta be nervous about it. Let me guess, you were a bouncer at the strip club she danced at, right?"

"Um...yeah, guilty as charged."

"At least you had a job. That's nothin' to be ashamed of. I loved my cousin, but I didn't know her that well. I'm Dawn."

"Andre."

"Nice to meet you, Andre. You're tall."

"A little."

"How many babies you claim on your W-2?"

"Ha, ha-ha, ha-ha! I don't have any babies."

"Oh, really? Interesting. You're a straight man, right?"

"I am indeed."

"Then, how can you stand here this long and not ask me for my number?"

"Oh, um...I was trying to be smooth."

"You failed there, Andre."

Quashon Davis

"Well, Dawn, can I have your number so I can give you a call sometime?"

"Why yes, Andre," she says, swiping his phone and putting her number in it.

"I'll call you."

"I know," she says, walking away.

***

Jay bursts through the doors at Lenox Hills Hospital. He's rushing down the hall to the front desk. Everyone he passes stops in their tracks as they recognize him. He doesn't slow down until he reaches the reception desk.

"What room is Roger Merrit in?" he asks.

"You're Jay Jones," the women all say, grinning.

"Please, just tell me what room Roger Merrit is in."

"Sorry. He's in room 1127."

Jay runs down the hall to Roger's room and throws the door open. He rushes in to see Roger being stitched up. He's lying on his back, looking extremely uncomfortable. There's an ugly open wound on one side of his stomach, and the doctor is halfway done stitching the wound on the opposite side.

"Dammit, Raj, I told you not to do this."

"I'm good, Jay. It's not as bad as it looks."

"It's not? You have two holes in your stomach. How is that not that bad?"

"I saw her, Jay. I looked right at her."

"Okay, so who is she?"

"I don't know. Her face was covered. I saw her eyes though."

"Oh, well then, why don't you put out an APB on those eyes, then?"

"Come on, Jay. Think about it. Last time I was hunting The Ghost, it took two years to get this close. I almost had her today."

"*This* is almost? Come on, Raj. You had a nice life in Brazil. You had money, nobody was lookin' for you. I just don't understand why you came back."

"I had *your* money, Jay. I had a life that wasn't mine. I wasn't even using my real name."

"You were safe though. You could live like a king down there. Why come back, Raj? Why?"

"Jay, I solved every case the department gave me. I was damn good. I was unstoppable. The cops used to place bets to see how fast I could solve cases. One day, a case came across my desk. A diplomat was visiting the UN from Vienna. It was some sort of summit. Fritz Goeth had his hands in a lot of bad things with a lot of bad people. Nobody knew that, though. He came to New York with his family for the summit. The bastard didn't even know the feds were onto him. A diplomat...a guy that people trusted and loved, and he was probably the biggest cocaine distributor in Europe. There's no honor in the drug game, bro. There was an up and coming dealer in Europe named Romey Strauss. Strauss was making money, but he wanted the territories that Goeth was dealing in. He was making good money, but he wanted great money. Strauss decided to do the only thing he could think of. He took eight million and paid The Ghost to assassinate Goeth. It's the only blemish The Ghost has on her record."

"Can you turn over for me, Detective Merrit?" the doctor requests.

"Sure."

So, yeah...Jay, anyway, she set up Goeth by planting an explosive in his cell phone. She showed up at his hotel and pretended to be there to fix something in his room. She planted the explosive on his phone and it worked perfectly. He was

Quashon Davis

killed instantly the moment he tried to use his phone. The Ghost made a mistake though. When she was in the hotel room, Goeth's son saw her messing with his phone. He knew what she looked like. I met with the kid. He was scared to death. He wouldn't talk, no matter what I asked him. I could tell that he wanted to, but the shock left him mute. I was bonding with him though, and he would smile every time he saw me. I just needed time. He was gonna describe her, man, I know he was.

"It was a Wednesday night, we just had pizza together, and I was about to head home. The kid took me by the hand. I knew it was his way of saying he didn't want me to leave yet. I stayed and played with the kid for two more hours, putting together Legos. I told him I'd be back in the morning and he finally said, 'Bye, Roger.' That's when I knew the next day, he would be ready to finally talk, give me The Ghost's description. I got there the next morning right after breakfast. The feds were there, crime scene techs, and everything was taped off. I fought my way through to see what was going on, but I already knew. I didn't want to see him, but I forced myself to. It took me a long time to work my way past the cops, FBI, and every other suit that was there investigating. Finally, I saw him. There he was. The kid was slumped over in his chair. I lost it, man. The Ghost poisoned his breakfast. He was nine, bro. After I got over the shock, I started thinking about the whole thing. How did The Ghost know the kid was about to talk? Was her timing a coincidence? Naw, nothing The Ghost does is coincidence. She was watching the kid and waiting. She killed a child because he saw her face. As good as I was, Jay, I wasn't good enough to stop her. I picture that boy's face every morning. I haven't really had breakfast since the day that child had his last one. I got close to her. I will catch her. She's gonna pay for all the people she's killed."

"You never told me that before."

"I know. I don't like talking about it. Hopefully that helps you understand why I need to do this."

"Raj, you don't have control of the situation. You're hurt. It could be worse next time."

"Or, I could catch her next time."

"It's not a game, man. You could be killed."

"If that's what it takes, I can deal with that."

"I can't."

"I got nothin', Jay. I lost my wife, I don't have any kids, both of my parents are long gone, it's just me. The job is my longest relationship. The Ghost is the only drama I ever had in that relationship. I gotta make it right."

"Dammit, Raj. I can't lose you, bro. We're brothers."

"That's why you hafta back me on this."

"You make me sick."

"That means you understand. I know you."

"What about my son, Raj? He needs his uncle."

"I know. I'm here for him. I can win this, Jay. I can beat her."

"I believe you, Raj. How long you gonna be stuck here?"

"Me? I'm leaving as soon as I get stitched up."

"No, you're not. You're staying here at least two days," says the doctor.

"You heard him, bro."

"I don't have two days."

"You do. You don't have a choice. I'm gonna stay here with you, bro."

"Great."

***

Quashon Davis

A few days later, Dre is dropping off Dawn after their second date. They've hit it off pretty fast, and both dates have been amazing. First, he took her to a concert, followed by dinner and dancing. Tonight they kept it simple by going to Dave & Buster's and competing against each other. As busy as Dre's schedule is, he keeps trying to carve out time to spend with Dawn. Her confidence and attitude work for him in a major way. It's been a while since he actually liked someone. She gives him a big passionate kiss before getting out of the car. Dre watches her walk all the way to her door. Once she goes inside, Dre pulls off, heading for the highway. Before he can reach the entrance, he sees police lights in his rearview mirror.

You gotta be kidding.

He reluctantly pulls over and turns his car off. He takes out his license and registration and waits patiently. Instead of the officer coming over to his window, he makes his way to the passenger side and gets in Dre's car. Dre looks over, disgusted, but not surprised. He stares at Reyes, who stares back at him without saying anything. They sit in silence for a few moments, just sizing each other up.

"This is harassment, Reyes."

"Not at all, you were driving erratically. Have you been drinking?"

"What do you want now, Reyes?"

"Me? Nothing. I just wanted to know if you came to your senses yet. Are you ready to talk to me?"

"We don't have anything to talk about."

"I think we do."

"You gonna follow me around, wasting your time, forever?"

"Nah. If you don't have anything to say, I'll leave you alone."

"I don't have anything to say, Reyes."

"Fine. I caught the tail end of your little date. She's a fine lookin' sista. She looks familiar, though. I couldn't think of where I knew her from. You know, it hit me, she's Tina's cousin. Tina Powell, you know the girl that was killed? Remember, you and your friends covered it up."

"Reyes, you gotta let this go. We didn't kill anyone, and we didn't cover anything up."

"Oh, okay. The cousin seems to like you. What's she gonna feel like when she finds out what you did to her cousin? You think you'll still get kisses like the one she just gave you?"

"Are you done, Reyes?"

"I guess so. You D & D guys really are heartless, man. Geez."

He gets out the car and leaves. Dre sits there disgusted for several minutes, before violently punching his dashboard.

***

In LaGuardia Airport's lobby for international returning flights, Roger stands patiently waiting. He's feeling pain where he was injured, but he's shrugging it off. He arrived an hour before Cian's plane was scheduled to arrive. In his mind, once he knows she's not on the plane, he knows she's The Ghost. There's no way she ever left. As the PA announces the flight's arrival, Roger prepares for his proof. He stands off to the side, fighting off anxiety. He's already trying to figure out where he should go to arrest Cian; her house, her gym, or maybe her job. As the passengers begin to walk into the lobby from the plane, Roger watches carefully and Roger smiles as there's no sign of Cian.

I knew it was her, he thinks.

As the last couple of people file from the plane, Roger has already turned around and began making his exit.

"Hey, don't I know you?" a voice says from over his shoulder.

Quashon Davis

He turns around to see Cian. She's standing with her suitcase, smiling at him.

"Hey, Roger, I remember you. You're Maya's friend. Dinner that night at R & B's. How you doin'?" she asks.

Roger is stunned to see her. His theory about her never leaving the country just went out the window.

"Cian, right? Hey, good to see you. What's goin' on?"

"Nothin' much. My job always has me traveling somewhere. I just want my shower and my bed. Whatchu doin' here?"

"Just handling some work stuff. You know how it is."

"I sure do. How's your friend, Jay?"

"He's okay. He doesn't change. The guy you met that night is always the exact same."

"Well, hopefully, he treats us to dinner again. That was fun."

"I'm sure he will."

"Well, you know I'm gonna tell Maya I saw you."

"Of course."

"Okay, take care."

"You too, Cian."

She walks away from Roger and he's as confused as ever. If Cian was out of the country, then who did he tangle with on the train? If Cian didn't kill Bengie, then he's back to square-one. As he sits there pondering, a thought comes to mind. Maybe she didn't get on the plane the day he watched her leave the house. *What if she pretended to leave that day and instead, left the country yesterday, and came back today?* He realizes he has too many thoughts in his head at one time. Maybe a long drive and a cronut will get his mind right.

***

101

SUSPECT BEHAVIOR

Joe arrives at the home of Juan Roso, a dynamic young pitcher for the Yankees. He's not sure what to expect, the call from the office just said he needed medical service fast. When he knocks on the door, he realizes he left his medical bag in the car. Joe lightly jogs down the stairs to his car when the door opens. There's Juan, a young, skinny twenty-year-old, worth more money than three-fourths of his country. His clothes are all torn, and his face and body look like he lost a fight. He's out of breath and looks as if he was up all night.

"Are you the doctor?" he asks frantically.

"I am. I'll be right there. I'm just grabbing my bag."

"Please hurry, sir," he pleads.

Joe quickly shuts his car door and runs up the stairs. He walks in the giant house and before he can ask what's wrong, he sees Juan's younger brother on the couch, bleeding profusely. He has open wounds on his arms and legs.

"Damn. What happened to him?" Joe asks.

Before he can answer, he sees something move from the corner of the room. Before he can comprehend what he's seeing, a tiger walks out from the corner to the middle of the room and stops. It sits down and watches Joe, Juan, and his brother. Joe is stunned and silent, standing there frozen in place, and the other two follow suit.

"Is that a damn tiger?" whispers Joe.

"When they delivered it this morning, they said it was trained. As soon as they left, it attacked us and started tearing up the place."

"It's a damn tiger," whispers Joe.

"I don't understand. They said it would listen."

"It's a damn *tiger*. It's only gonna listen to another damn tiger. Why the hell would you buy a damn tiger?" whispers Joe.

"I have money now. It seemed like the thing to do."

Quashon Davis

"You're an idiot. It's gonna eat us. Why would you call me here to be eaten with the two of you?"

"I called you to stitch us up. You can see we both need stitches."

"You shoulda waited 'til after the tiger killed you both to call me."

Joe slowly reaches into his bag and pulls out a syringe. The tiger begins growling and looking at them, while he quickly fills it with a tranquilizer.

"Is the tiger going to kill us?" whispers Juan's brother.

"Yes, he is. I just hope he prefers Mexican over European," Joe says, tapping the side of the syringe with his finger.

They watch as the tiger perks up and roars loudly. Before they can react, he runs over to them and bites into Juan's shoe, causing Juan to yell loudly as its teeth pierce his foot. Joe quickly plunges the needle into the side of the tiger and pushes the plunger down. The animal falls over, unconscious. Juan and his brother let out a sigh of relief.

"What the hell is wrong with you, man? Say you're gonna send that animal back or I'm gonna euthanize it right now," Joe blasts.

"I promise."

"I'm gonna need ten grand in cash from you, before I stitch the two of you up."

"Ok."

"Idiots."

***

Jay arrives at TLPSA to pick up James. He has to go to the bathroom, so he parks and heads over to the main building. When he gets there, the door is locked. He looks around, weighing his options, because he doesn't want to pee outside.

SUSPECT BEHAVIOR

He sees Ted trimming hedges, so he walks over and asks him where he can go. Ted tells him the gym is open, and should be empty. Jay jogs across the field toward it. Once he gets there, he realizes he should've asked Ted why the main office was locked. He walks in and relieves himself. The bathrooms at TLPSA are better than most wedding halls. They're clean, fancy, and even have video monitors in them. Jay washes his hands and as he grabs a paper towel, Sapphire is standing in the doorway. He looks at her, while continuing to dry his hands. She stares at him, never blinking. The two share an awkward, tension-filled minute of silence.

CHAPTER EIGHT
A MOTHER ALWAYS KNOWS

"He's my son, isn't he?"

"What?"

"Don't play dumb with me, Jay."

"What do you want?"

"I want you to tell me that James is my son."

"Why would I tell you that?"

"Is this really how you want to play this? You want me to tell the world what you did? I know you. I know what the 'holier than thou,' good name of Jay Jones means to you."

"Listen, I don't know what you're trying to do here. I don't understand."

"You know, you almost got away with it. I really believed I miscarried that night. I didn't even question it. I was heartbroken, but I moved on. I just figured it wasn't meant for me to be a mother. You know when it changed for me? I saw your family on television at All-Star weekend. That boy didn't look like your wife at all. He had my ears and nose though. I didn't think too much about it, at first. I was out with some other folks after one of my concerts, and one of them mentioned their kid went to this school. We started talking about it, and guess who they said attended also? That's when I started researching. You did a decent job hiding him, but you never should've enrolled him here. This is a school for talented and gifted kids. It was probably your wife's idea and you couldn't come up with a reason good enough to say no. Once I saw him sing and play the piano, I knew right away. I don't know how you did it, but I know. James is my son and I want him back."

"Sapphire, what the hell? How you gonna just show up out the blue, talkin' crazy?"

"Crazy? Okay, I'll just go to the police then."

"Okay, okay. What? What do you want?"

"Admit he's my son."

"He's your son."

There's a long pause. Tears pour down Sapphire's face. Jay looks ashamed, and doesn't know what to do. He looks down at the ground and shakes his head lightly, while stuffing his hands in his pockets.

"How did you do it, Jay?"

"Come on, there's no need to—"

"How did you do it?"

"I paid the doctor. You and Shel were at the hospital, in labor at the same time. She miscarried, you didn't. You were both high-risk. They had to put y'all to sleep. When you gave birth, we switched him with…the other one—"

"The dead one, you mean?"

"Yes."

"Because, Jay Jones, the man that every woman loves and every man wants to be, couldn't be labeled as the man who cheated on his girl and got someone pregnant. I get it."

"Listen, I'm sorry. I didn't know what to do. I just, I don't know."

Quashon Davis

"You're sorry? You have the whole world fooled. Everyone thinks you're this great guy. You're a family man. You're always smiling, talking to fans, giving to charities, all that garbage. None of that is you. The *real* you is a monster. A monster that would destroy the world, if it meant preserving your precious image."

"What are you gonna do?"

"I'm gonna take *my* son. I'm gonna tell the world who you are, and what you are."

"Sapphire, I know you're upset, but you're not thinking clearly. Like it or not, you need to consider what's best for James. Telling him this now would break his heart. He would be very confused. Why don't we make an agreement, where you get some visitation and he doesn't know the truth?"

"Doesn't know the truth? Are you standing there telling me, we should keep this on the low to preserve *your* name? Don't tell *my* son that *I'm* his mother? You got a set on you, Jay Jones. Your precious name is gone. Your empire is mine. The world is gonna know what you did, your wife is gonna know what you did, while the two of you were engaged. *Our* son is gonna know what kind of man you really are."

"I'm a good father. I understand you're upset, but my back was against the wall. I couldn't figure out what else to do. Come on, you know that's too much to lay on a four-year-old. I handled it wrong and I'm sorry. There has to be a way to work this out."

"Work this out, huh? You could explain to your wife what you did. You can tell our son that I'm his mom. You can get ready to pay me a chunk of that six-hundred-million-dollar empire you're sitting on. I can't believe I thought you were a good guy."

"Sapphire, I know you don't want to hear this, but James is very happy with the parents he has. You can expose me, drag

107

us into court, make it a spectacle, he's still not gonna want to be with you."

"Of course, he is. He's my son. Of course, he'll want to be with me."

"I know you want to tell the world on me, but why don't you just give it a few days? Think this over. This is a lot to process. I know you're mad, but look at your schedule, seriously. You're all over the world performing three hundred days a year. You're gonna take him and have a nanny raise him, while you're off working all the time? Shel and I are home with him every night. I help him with homework, Shel tucks him in. When would you do those things?"

"I-I don't need you to try and figure out my schedule. You have a week to tell your family what's going on."

"Saph, come on."

"Don't call me that. I'll be in touch. Make sure you tell your family what's going on before the next time you hear from me."

Sapphire walks out of the bathroom. Jay stands there for several minutes, looking at himself in the mirror. He knows he's in trouble. The stress is forming on his face. He knows he has to get it together and think.

"Damn, what am I gonna do now? Shel is gonna leave me, if she doesn't kill me first. James is her life...my life. What the hell are my teammates gonna say? My fans? The tabloids are gonna have a field day with this. I can see it now. Golden boy, Jay Jones, is just like every other dirty athlete."

In his frustration, he slams his hands down on the counter.

A sudden and painful headache forms in seconds, right in the front of his brain. His stomach knots up as if he's waiting in line for a rollercoaster. For a moment, he feels dizzy. The lights in the room go from dim to bright.

"Roger, I'll call Roger. He'll help me."

Quashon Davis

He stumbles out and dials Roger.

"Jay, I got a lot goin' on over here, bro. Can I call you back?"

"I just saw Sapphire."

"What? Where?"

"At James' school."

"What the hell was she doing there?"

"She knows, Raj. She knows James is hers."

"What's she trying to do?"

"She wants him. She said she's gonna tell everyone what I did."

"Damn. That's not good. What are you gonna do?"

"I don't know, man. I don't know what to do."

"Listen, bro, I know how much the world loves you, but that's about to be over. You're gonna be the ultimate villain. You need to prepare yourself for it. People are gonna look at you and roll their eyes. Kids aren't gonna be wearing your jersey anymore. It's gonna be a lot, bro."

"There has to be something I can do."

"You can keep trying to reason with her. That's about it."

"Maybe I will. You said you were busy, what's up?"

"My Ghost theory hit a snag. I haven't given up, though."

"You know, Raj, you're supposed to be this great detective. I can't believe I need to give you work advice."

"I'll take it, bro. Whatchu got?"

"You said she charges eight million per kill, right?"

"That's right."

"I'm guessing not too many folks have eight million bucks lying around. Have you tried following the money?"

"That's good advice, actually. The problem is that there's no money to follow. We don't know who's paying, or who's getting paid. There's no starting point. We don't even know how people hire The Ghost. I'm sure she makes herself accessible to people with a lot of money."

"I'll see if any of my hoity-toity friends know anything."

"Thanks, Jay. I'll call you tonight. Try not to worry. I know you're all stressed out."

"Of course I am, Shel's gonna rip my lips off."

"Yeah, she is, but she won't leave you."

"I hope not."

"Man, come on. Nine out of ten men would smash Sapphire if they had the chance, no matter what situation they're in."

"Yeah, that's exactly what I'm gonna tell Shel when it hits the fan."

"Ha, ha-ha, ha-ha! I'll call you later, bro."

"A'ight."

***

Roger begins poring over all of The Ghost's past victims, making the connections to their friends, enemies, families. If he can find one person who's contracted The Ghost, he'll know how it's done. He spends the next several hours, poring over information. Everything is a dead end. The Ghost doesn't leave any breadcrumbs. After twenty hours of looking over old cases, he comes across a file for Angus Thompson, a man accused of raping the young daughter of a business tycoon in London. While Angus was awaiting trial, he was mysteriously killed. He was found in a laundromat poisoned to death. There were no witnesses, and the CCTV footage was erased. No one saw anyone go in or out. He was poisoned with a synthetic toxin, something too sophisticated for the average person to make.

Quashon Davis

The rich tycoon whose daughter was raped is Rupert Hastings, a borderline billionaire who has built a Fortune 500 computer company. His daughter is an eighteen-year-old college freshman now. They still live in London where his company is based. Roger calls Jay and asks him if he can use his jet. Within an hour, Roger is on his way to London to talk to Hastings.

He hasn't been in Jay's private jet since he had to flee the country. Sitting in it brings back a lot of old memories. The last person he saw when he got in the plane the last time was Miesha. He's thought about calling her every day since he got back. He left with so many questions. There was a lot left unsaid, and he wonders every day how she feels about it. He's let his anger control him for years regarding the situation, but Roger still loves Miesha. When he thinks about her, before the thoughts of her and his ex-partner sneaking around behind his back surface, there's all the positivity and fun he had with her. She was his first love, and she was what men refer to as a unicorn. She was a big football fan, loved superhero movies, and handled her business in every aspect of home life.

He pretended to be unfazed regarding her affair with Marie, but he was broken. He got to Brazil a defeated shell. He was a fugitive. Miesha chose his ex-partner over him basically. He lost his badge, his life, and himself. For weeks, he wandered around the streets of Brazil like a homeless man. Jay had bought him a nice place to live, but he stayed on the streets, depressed. The homeless people took him in, and even though he didn't talk much, they considered him family. In typical Roger fashion, when one of his new homeless buddies was robbed and beaten, he not only figured out who did it, but beat them pretty bad and retrieved the man's items.

After six months of living on the street, he took his five new homeless buddies and moved them into the house Jay bought for him. They cleaned up and eventually, just by saving the money Jay was sending him monthly, he bought them a

111

small restaurant. By the time Roger got the call to come back to the U.S., the Vagrant Pub was one of the hottest spots in Brazil, and its five owners owed him everything.

Reminiscing about the past always brings him back to Miesha. He takes out his phone and looks at her name. He's done this several times, but he never presses send. He just wants to hear her voice so bad. She has to still feel something. Roger takes a deep breath, and presses send. The ringing sound seems to go on forever. The lump in his throat gets bigger and bigger.

"Hello?"

"Esh...hey, it's me."

"Raj? You got a lot of nerve calling. What did you do to Marie?"

"We had a little fight."

"Since when do you fight women? I don't know who you are anymore."

"I get that. Yeah, I beat Marie down for the whole thing. So what? Can we not talk about that?"

"You are amazing. The nerve you have. Why are you back in the country?"

"They needed me on a case. I've been back for a while. I'm headed to London though to track down a lead."

"You got pardoned for shooting Pete? Well, I guess that's good for you."

"I appreciate that. It's uh...good to hear your voice."

"You put your hands on Marie, Roger. Save it!"

"Okay, maybe I didn't handle it the best. I'm sorry. I've been holding that anger in for a long time."

"I'm sure you have. I guess you think that makes it right."

"You're still with Marie, though?"

Quashon Davis

"We're in the same house. I went into a depression when you left the country. Jay was always like a brother to me, but he stopped speaking to me. I didn't know what to do. People that I've known my whole life cut me off. My own parents cursed me out over you. I've had to live with all that since you left. Marie really cares about me and I know it but honestly, I've wanted her to leave for a long time. It just feels like if I say it, it officially becomes a complete waste. Almost like the Kyrie trade. You trade him for Isiah Thomas, who's nowhere near as good as him. Even though that's bad, once you trade Thomas away, now you officially lost Kyrie for nothing."

"That's why you're a unicorn."

"Wait a minute, what kind of case could be so important that they would pardon you?"

"I can't really get into it."

"Don't give me that. I've known you your entire adult life. What kind of case is it?"

"The Ghost is in New York City, taking out some high-profile targets. They need me to take care of it."

"You must be kidding. That person almost killed you a few years back. You began losing your mind. You went two weeks without sleep. Don't tell me you're gonna go through that again."

"That was a long time ago. I can catch her. It's gonna be different this time."

"She's gonna kill you, Raj."

"She won't."

"Well, be careful. Even though you abuse women now, I wouldn't want to see you get hurt, I guess."

"I'll call you when I get back from London."

"Well, be as safe as you can, Raj."

"I will."

"I'll talk to you soon. Bye."

113

"Bye, Esh."

Roger smiles to himself and sits back in his chair. It's a long flight to London and he might as well try to get some sleep.

***

Damon walks into Dante's office, closes the door and sits down. Reyes has been after them for a long time, but he seems to be getting closer and closer to achieving his goal. Although they've considered him to be a joke for years, he's enough of a threat now to have a private meeting.

"We've been doin' our thing for years now. Reyes has been after us since day-one. Why should we be worried now?" Damon asks.

"He's an idiot, but he's gotten close a few times recently. Our luck is gonna run out eventually. The reason we make so much money, is because every professional athlete wants us to represent them. The reason they do goes far beyond the average agent and athlete relationship. We're urban legends. They've heard the stories. D & D, the agency that got a guy out of six DUI's. They once had a guy that passed a drug test while he was high. They had a client that was involved in a drive-by shooting, and everyone went to jail, except him."

"Even though he was the shooter," laughs Damon.

"Exactly. Those stories are why athletes come to us. They need us. If we were out of the game, half of them would be locked up. Reyes almost caught us slippin' a couple of times this month. We need to get out ahead of it."

"How, Dante?"

"Easy. He's an idiot. Have somebody follow him for a couple of days. I'm sure he cheats on his wife, or has something he doesn't want anyone to know. Once we know what it is, we'll blackmail him."

"Why don't we just pay him to look the other way?"

Quashon Davis

"We could, but he's annoying. He doesn't deserve our money, Damon. I'd rather force him to leave us alone."

"You're the boss. Who do you want on it?"

"Give it to Veronica."

"Didn't she say call her Ronnie?"

"Man, just give it to her."

"Okay."

"And we're both the boss, kinda."

"Yeah, whatever."

"Damon, remember when we were living on the streets and we talked about being millionaires?"

"Of course. We were a couple of stick-up kids. We dreamed about fancy cars and lots of money,"

"Hell, yeah. We always said nice guys don't get to have that life."

"I know. What about Jay, though? He always took care of us."

"He's the exception. Me and you, we said it then and it stands true today, we do what we gotta do to survive."

"Amen, brotha."

CHAPTER NINE
THE BIG TIP

KENSINGTON IS THE MOST EXPENSIVE area to live in all of London. On a brightly lit corner, sits the mansion of Rupert Hastings. The business tycoon is sitting in his living room, drinking his pre-dinner tea when his doorbell rings. Hastings doesn't even flinch. He continues sipping and reading the paper. His butler comes out from the kitchen and opens the door.

"May I help you, sir?"

"Yes. I'm Detective Roger Merrit from New York City. I'm here because I need to talk to Rupert Hastings."

"I'm sorry, sir. Master Hastings is only available during business hours. You would have to visit the office and make an appointment."

"Tell him I'm here to talk about June thirtieth of last year."

The butler turns toward where Hastings is sitting. He gives him a nod of approval. Roger walks in and he greets him, inviting him to sit down. The butler pours him some tea before Hastings orders him to give them privacy.

"What can I do for you, Roger Merrit of New York City?"

"I'm gonna be very honest with you. I don't have time for the sugar coating. The Ghost is in my city. Usually she goes to a location, takes out a target and disappears. There's something happening that's caused her to spend time in New York eliminating targets. I've been tasked with stopping her. Last year, you hired The Ghost to kill the man that raped your daughter. I know you did and I can prove it. I don't care about that. Honestly, I would've done the same thing. I need to know how you contacted her, and how you paid her. If you give me the information I'm asking for, I'll walk right back out that door, and you'll never see me again. I won't tell anyone where I got the information from, and you can go on drinking your unsweetened tea. If you don't give me the information I need, I'm gonna go to the police here and give them all the evidence I have. It's not much, so I'd hafta alert the local newspapers. Your precious stock would nosedive, you'll lose a lot of money, and you'll be drinking Lipton Brisk out of the can."

"You drive a hard bargain, Roger Merrit of New York City. I guess there's no sense in lying to you about it. Yes, I hired The Ghost. People with real money know how to get her attention. She has a system in place to protect her identity. I warn you, Detective, The Ghost has never missed a mark. No one is crazy enough to go after her. Are you certain you wish to go down this road?"

"I am."

"You have to understand, I'd do anything to protect my daughter. When she was raped, I felt like a failure. There was a chance that bastard was gonna get away with it. I couldn't let that happen. I'd always heard the stories about the globe-trotting assassin that never misses the mark. I started asking all my rich friends about it. Finally, my good friend, Helen, told me she would help. She caught her husband cheating with the maid. When she caught him, he tried to divorce her and take the fortune they'd made together. During the trial, he had a massive heart attack. I felt terrible for her. It was only when I was asking around about hiring The Ghost that she told me The Ghost was behind his 'heart attack.'"

SUSPECT BEHAVIOR

"Are you saying The Ghost can make killings look like they weren't killings?"

"Yes. Any way you want it to happen, The Ghost will do it. Hell, you're paying enough. Imagine how many killings The Ghost has done that no one will ever know about. How many faked accidents, suicides, heart attacks, even natural causes. Anyway, she gave me the information and I tried it. What you do is, you write on any social media, 'i need a vacation.' Your Facebook, Instagram, Snapchat, anything. You could even put it on your LinkedIn. The thing is…you don't capitalize the I. You keep it lowercase. If The Ghost thinks you have the money, and I'm sure she checks carefully first, she calls you. Don't get excited, Detective, she calls from a throw-away cell and the call lasts for twenty seconds. When you answer, there's a quick exchange. You give the name of the person you want killed, and she gives you an offshore account number. She hangs up after that. Once she hangs up, you have two minutes to transfer four million into the account she gives you. Once the person is killed, you have forty-eight hours to transfer the other half. She covers every base, my friend. You should let this go before she kills you."

"I appreciate the warning. I think I'll take my chances, though. Is there anything else you can tell me?"

"Sorry, Detective. When she hung up, Angus Thompson was dead within ten hours. I wired the rest of the money into the account and never heard anything else about it."

"Do you still have the account number?"

"Yes, I do."

"I need it."

"I will give it to you. When The Ghost tortures you, do not say my name."

"I won't. I promise."

Quashon Davis

"Good. Would you like some filet mignon? You might as well stay for dinner. Ivan has prepared a wonderful meal, and he always makes too much."

"My plane isn't scheduled to go back for a couple of hours, so count me in. You gotta bring me some sugar for this tea, though."

***

Joe calls his ex-wife on his way to his apartment. With more cash than he's had in a long time, he's excited to spend some time with his kids. Unfortunately for him, his ex likes to use his kids to frustrate him. She refuses to let him see them, no matter how much he begs. She tells him if he has a job where he's making money now, she'll be going down to city hall to increase his child support payment. Frustrated, he hangs up on her as he arrives at his place. His trunk full of children's toys will have to wait. He turns on the television and pours himself a bowl of cereal. Not being able to see his daughters is taking a toll on him. He kicks his shoes off and tries to focus on the TV. He can't get his little girls' smiling faces off his mind. They must be extremely disappointed in him. If only they knew it was their mother and not him. He's tried to do the right thing for so long, it gets exhausting. He takes some deep breaths, and slaps the cereal bowl to the floor. With his head is in his hands, tears start to flow. Finally, he takes a small silver case from his pocket and places down some rows of cocaine. It's been a long time. He snorts a couple of lines and sits back slowly on the couch, massaging his nose.

***

Across town, Dre is sitting in the park facing the ocean. He's looking at a picture of Tina Powell on his phone. He feels a tear come down, then another. The guilt is tearing him apart. On top of that, he's keeping everything from Dawn, who he is really starting to like. He keeps imagining when he walked up to Tina's car. She had the most innocent face. She was sweet and polite. He could've just offered her five grand, but because he liked her spirit so much, he offered her eight. The first thing she said to him that night was could he call 911 for her. He talked her out of it. If he didn't, she'd probably still be alive. When he's home, it feels like he's being haunted. He sees her everywhere. Dre feels like a murderer, and it's a feeling that doesn't seem to be going away anytime soon. He wipes his face and tries to relax. Dawn walks up and kisses him on the cheek.

"There's my tall man."

"Hey, Dawn."

"What's wrong? You look sad."

"Ah, nothin'. I'm just having one of those days."

"Well, you know you can talk to me about anything. I hope you know that."

"I do."

"So, what's up? Talk to me, Dre."

***

Inside the thick walls of the giant institution, Sing Sing prison, there are currently more than two thousand inmates. The facility derived its name from the Native American tribe, Sinck Sinck, who they purchased the land from in 1685. The old building that was built in 1826 has housed infamous killers like David Berkowitz aka the Son of Sam, and Albert Fish aka the Werewolf of Wysteria. The fifth prison built in New York City, its famous electric chair called "Old Sparky," executed 614 men and women, up until 1972.

It is here that young R.J. comes every week to see Robert Johnson, Senior, his forty-five-year-old father, who is serving a life sentence. Ten years ago, Senior was at a party with his friends and one of them got into a fight. Robert punched a man who fell and hit his head. That man died, and he got a forty-five-year sentence. One of the things that keeps him going is hearing about R.J.'s success. He looks forward to seeing him every week. R.J. tells him stories all the time about the clients D & D deals with, and it is great entertainment. Today, however, R.J. comes into the visiting room in a different mood. He looks worried. The guards open the doors and his father walks in. The short man with massive arms smiles with pride when he sees the kid that looks just like him. He can tell something is wrong, though. He picks up the phone, concerned.

"What's up, son?"

"Hey, Pop. How's it goin' in there?"

"I don't have ESPN, but I'm gettin' through it. You look like something is up. Talk to me."

"I'm having some issues at work."

"I have people on the outside. You need somebody to get hurt?"

"No, Pop…nothing like that."

"Okay, so what's goin' on?"

"You know what we do at my company."

"Yeah, I think it's great. I'm proud of what you do."

"Well, not everyone is. There's this cop, he's been trying to bring the company down for a long time. He came to my house and said he was close. He told me if I didn't want to go to jail for the rest of my life, tell him everything I know and he'll keep me out of jail."

"Do you think he's close?"

"He gets closer every day."

"Tell him everything."

"Huh?"

"Tell him to put it in writing that you'll get immunity and tell him everything."

"Pop, how can you say that? You're in the 'no-snitch' capital of the world."

"That's why I can say it. Son, you still have a long life to live. You're smart, young, and I know you got a nice savings account. You can find another job easily. Do you know what my day is like? I get up, have breakfast, lift weights and avoid skinheads. Then, I have lunch, lift weights, avoid skinheads, have dinner, lift weights, avoid skinheads, and go to bed. That's been my schedule for ten years. Think about that. That's seven days a week, three hundred and sixty-five days a year. And, I have thirty-five more years to go. My life is over, son. I knew that at thirty-five. I won't see freedom again until I'm eighty years old. I don't want this life for you. You're smart as hell. You always were. When you were born, I was out there on those streets sellin' drugs twenty-four hours a day, to make sure you wouldn't have to pay for college when you were ready to go. I didn't do that so you could be in here. Trust me, there's nothin' but broken dreams up in here. My cell mate is the brother of that famous basketball player. Your guy that y'all represent. He's in here for rape. The guy must be six-eight. I hear his big ass gettin' raped every week. I gotta watch my back in here twenty-four-seven. I don't want this life for you. If you gotta snitch on some folks to stay out, do it."

"I aint no snitch, Pop."

"You aint no thug either. Think about that."

"Come on."

"I'm serious. Whatchu gonna do when a giant thug takes your dinner tray? You gonna beat him down and take it back? You gonna go to bed hungry? You go to bed hungry once, you will for years."

"I get it Pop."

"I hope so. You ain't bout this life. Do what you gotta do, son."

Quashon Davis

R.J. walks out of the prison and heads towards his car. He takes his phone out and checks his messages. As he reaches into his pocket for his car key, he looks up and sees Reyes standing by his car.

"You have got to be kidding me."

"Mr. Johnson. How's it going, sir? Fancy running into you here."

"This is harassment."

"What do you mean? I was here to do some inspections, fill out some reports, and I just happened to run into you."

"Whatever, man. You're wasting your time."

"Am I? You know, you look just like him. You got the same face. You know the difference? You still have that confidence in your face. That was stripped away from him. His arms, his attitude, his skills, he's fine in there. You, on the other hand, wouldn't last a month. You ready to talk?"

"Reyes, you're chasing ghosts. You know that D & D isn't dirty."

"When it goes down, every employee is going to jail, except whoever gives me the information I need. I hope you're that guy, R.J. I really do."

He quickly gets in his car and speeds away. Reyes watches him run the red light and smiles wide.

***

Inside the large, full-sized basketball court Jay has in his home, he's shooting basketballs from the three-point line. This is his version of stress relief. Shot after shot, he never misses. Everyone has different ways of dealing with stress. Some people clean, some exercise, Jay just shoots a thousand shots. The muscle memory and repetition cause him to get into an astonishing rhythm. He has to be somewhere around sixty straight makes. In another wing of his home, Shel and their child are playing. They're laughing and enjoying each other, with no idea their lives are on the verge of being turned upside down. As he continues to hit shot after shot, Jay wonders if he's going to end up losing both his wife and his son. In hindsight, he probably should've told Shel the truth from the beginning. Unfortunately for him, Sapphire was right. His name means everything to him.

Ever since he was a child, Jay was considered a really good kid. His twin brother was the bad one. Jay was the kid that ate his veggies, did his homework, and made his bed. He was an A-student and tutored other kids, even on the weekends. In high school, he was the number-one player in the country his junior and senior year. He was still an A-student, and still tutored other kids. Everyone looked up to him. He never got in trouble, never broke rules, and was a role model to everyone. His time in the NBA was brief, but he made the most of it. Besides the championships and MVP awards, he was the humanitarian of the year four times. He never succumbed to the low-hanging trouble fruit that many men in professional sports go after.

To this day, if you ask anyone about Jay Jones, they're going to tell you he's a great guy. She was right in saying his name does mean everything to him. He's never been a villain. He doesn't want that to change. As his phone begins to ring, Jay presses the button on his headphones and continues shooting.

"Hello?"

"Jay, what's up, bro?"

"Dante? Hey, what's goin' on? I haven't talked to you in a while."

"I know, man. You know we got a lot goin' on. I know you hate retirement. You ready for me to make that call? I can get you back in the league."

"Ha! I'm good, bro. I wear house shoes all day every day. I ain't goin' back."

"Well, you made me enough money. I could live off the ten percent from your sneaker sales for the rest of my life."

"How's Damon?"

"He's good, man. You know he's always workin' on something."

"Yeah, I know. Okay, Dante, tell me what's goin' on."

"Whatchu mean?"

"I know you, man. I've been bailing you and Damon outta trouble since the Big Brother program. Talk to me."

"D & D is in trouble. We've made enough money, that ain't the problem. It's this cop, Reyes. He's been on us for a while and he's gettin' close to finding some evidence to nail us."

"Evidence?"

"Jay, it's best if you don't know. Let's just say...remember that little car accident you had us make happen years ago with that singer's personal assistant? Well, we've done much worse things to protect clients. We've had situations where people actually got hurt."

"You're right, I don't wanna know. I know Reyes though, he ain't Roger. He's not that good of a detective."

"That's why we're still okay. He's an idiot, driven though. I think we may be on thin ice, though."

"What do you want me to do?"

"Talk to Raj. Tell him this guy, Reyes, is all over us. We've known him as long as we've known you, even though he doesn't know us that well."

"I'll see what I can do, bro."

"Thanks, Jay. I appreciate it. How's Shel and James?"

"They're good, man. Stop being so busy and come by for dinner one night. James thinks he can beat you at thumb-wrestling now."

"I will, bro, I promise. It's gonna slow down over here soon."

"Okay, I'll talk to Raj and see what he says."

"Thanks. Later, bro."

"Later."

As soon as he hangs up with Dante, his phone rings again.

"Yeah,"

"Hey, bro. You busy?"

"Raj. Naw, I'm chillin', bro. What happened out there? You find out anything?"

"Yeah, I did. I'm on the way back now. I need your help, though."

""Sure, whatchu need?"

"This guy gave me the offshore account number that he put the money in to pay The Ghost for the hit."

"That's great."

"It is. I don't wanna take it to the department yet, though."

"Why?"

"I know the feds. They'll take the info, take the case from me, and blow it. The Ghost will be in the wind and I'll never catch her."

"Okay, so what do you want me to do?"

"You still good with computers?"

"Sure."

"I'm gonna send you the offshore account number. Find out who or what that account is linked to. When I get back, I'm coming to you."

"I gotchu, bro, later."

CHAPTER TEN
THE UNEXPECTED DENTAL EMERGENCY

JOE IS SITTING IN HIS car, eating a cheap-looking breakfast sandwich. He looks like he hasn't slept in days. The bags under his eyes are thick and heavy. There's an open bottle of Jack Daniels in his cup holder. Debris from his breakfast litters his moustache. In between bites, Joe snorts lines of cocaine. He's called his ex-wife three times today, but he can't get an answer. Without his girls, the money he's making makes no difference to him. Joe takes a swig of Jack and tries to think about something else.

He gets a text on his phone to go to a familiar place, the home of Jack Bixby, the abusive NFL offensive lineman. He's already been there twice to provide medical assistance to women that Bixby hurt. The job has been more difficult than he expected, but he doesn't want to lose it. With this kind of money, whenever his ex finally stops being difficult, he'll be ready. He reluctantly starts the car. After one more sip, he pulls off and heads to Bixby's. He's coming to a strange revelation. Before he got this job, he was home all the time. D & D has given him a feeling, a purpose. He felt like a loser before this job. Could it be that the job is all he has?

While he's driving, he tries calling his ex-wife again, but he gets the same result. The frustration is getting to him. His ex-wife never worked. When he was a prominent doctor, she was a housewife. After his drug problem and subsequent job loss, he was ordered to pay a lot of child support. Before D & D, he was paying her and struggling to live. Ironically, now he's making a lot of money and without his daughters, he's struggling to live. The morning sun is fighting with his face to sober him up. He parks in front of the house and begins taking deep breaths. He takes another swig of Jack and grabs his medical bag. Joe slowly walks up to the familiar door. Before he rings the bell, the door opens. Bixby's frame takes up the entire doorway. He looks Joe up and down with annoyance on his face.

"I called them over an hour ago. You guys sure do take your time," says Bixby.

Joe walks in and sees a woman sitting on the floor with a black eye. Her lip is busted and looks like it needs to be stitched up. Joe looks up in the air in an attempt to calm his nerves.

"I had her sit on the floor, Doc. I didn't wanna mess up my couch, you know?"

Joe ignores him and walks over to the woman while opening his medical bag. He begins cleaning all her cuts and scrapes.

"You do good work, Doc. I meant to tell you that," says Bixby.

"I need eighty-five hundred, cash," Joe replies.

"You're all business, huh? No problem. It's already on the counter. Drop her off at the bus stop when you're done."

Bixby begins to walk up his stairs, when he hears Joe's voice.

"You're the biggest coward I've ever seen."

"What did you say?"

Quashon Davis

"It takes a six-five, three-hundred-fifty-pound man to hurt a woman? How can you put your hands on innocent, defenseless women? I just don't get it."

"Oh, yeah? How about I come over there and put my hands on you? Hell, it'll probably be easier."

"You're the worst type of man. You outweigh these women by two-hundred-fifty pounds."

"You're not gonna come into my house and disrespect me. I'm gonna hurt you!"

Bixby runs up to Joe while he's helping the woman. He snatches him by his shirt and throws him across the room. Joe lands hard and quickly realizes he's in trouble. Bixby comes stomping over to him and kicks him in the stomach while he's on the floor. Joe struggles to his feet and punches Bixby, who shrugs it off and throws him again. The woman begins screaming. Joe gets to his feet and quickly looks around for something he can use as a weapon. Bixby interrupts his search with a punch to the jaw that sends him flying again. Joe feels dizzy and he's stumbling around, trying to shake off the cobwebs. Bixby punches him again, sending him to the ground.

"Even though you've probably learned your lesson, I think I'll cut you so you always remember," he says, taking a knife from the kitchen.

He charges at Joe, who avoids a couple of wild swings with the kitchen knife. He quickly reaches down and picks up his medical bag, swinging it and knocking the knife out of Bixby's hand. He grabs Joe by the throat and lifts him off his feet. Joe is struggling to get his breath. The room is beginning to get dark. His mind is in overload. *I can't believe I'm going out this way.* He thinks about his daughters. As sad as it is, they've been growing up without a father. This is going to make that permanent. After he finally has a job making real money, he's going to die. His ex told him cocaine was going to kill him. Of course, as soon as he goes back for a taste, it looks like it's

129

about to be over. As he struggles for air, he tries to think about his family instead of death. He concentrates on them, instead of the gurgling sounds he's making.

"Die, you cheap quack!" Bixby demands.

Out of nowhere, the expensive guitar he keeps on the wall crashes into the back of Bixby's head. He drops Joe and turns around to see the scared woman he abused, holding just the broken tip of the guitar. He slaps her down to the floor and jumps on her, choking her.

"You little bitch!"

As he chokes the woman, Bixby feels a pain in his back like nothing he's ever felt before. He immediately knows there's something wrong. He reaches for his back, but can't get to where the pain is. He turns around and sees Joe standing there. He immediately realizes the knife is stuck in his back. He tries to reach it for a few seconds before realizing he can't. He decides since that's not working, to just beat on Joe some more. Unfortunately for him, when he grabs Joe he feels all of his strength leave his body. His legs go numb and his vision begins to fade. Bixby's lifeless body hits the floor, sounding like a piano hitting a New York street. Joe goes over and checks on the woman, before the scope of what had just happened hits him.

"This is really bad," he says.

"Is...that man dead?" the woman asks.

"Yes, he is," Joe says, while checking his pulse.

"Oh my God."

Joe quickly calls Dante to tell him what happened. Within twenty minutes Dante, Damon and Dre arrive at Bixby's house. They park the car a block away and walk. When they walk in, they know right away they're in deep trouble. Looking around, the place is trashed, and there's broken glass and wood everywhere. Blood is staining the floor and walls. For the first time, Dante actually looks a little nervous. He and Damon are surveying the damage, while Dre is standing in front of Bixby's lifeless body, looking terrified.

"This is really bad," says Dre.

"Yeah, it is. I think you actually undersold this on the phone," Dante says.

"Are you okay?" asks Damon.

"Yeah, I'm okay."

"Um...who's the girl?" asks Dante.

"That's Asia. I was in the middle of helping her when he attacked me."

"Damn. We can't...okay, okay. Asia, we're gonna trust you not to say anything about this. Let me see your license," Damon requests.

Still shaking, she goes over to her purse and gets the ID out and hands it to Damon. He takes it and puts it in his pocket.

"You can go," he says.

She can't get out the door fast enough. Asia kisses Joe on the cheek before stumbling out the door.

"Okay, now what?" asks Dre.

"Dante, call the dentist," Damon says.

"Man, come on."

"D, I'm not touching that guy. Make the call, bro."

"You gonna pay the dentist?"

"Man, stop playing. We got plenty of money. Call," Damon demands.

"Who the hell is the dentist?" asks Joe.

"Just a guy," Dante says, dialing the number.

"Dentist's office," the voice says.

"I need an extraction and a major cleaning," Dante requests.

"Address?"

"It's four-thirty-one Llewellyn Place."

"How many teeth?"

"One."

"That's gonna be twenty-five thousand, cash only. The dentist will be there in twenty minutes." the voice says, hanging up.

"I don't think we have that much cash," Dre says.

"No, we don't," Dante says, handing everyone latex gloves.

"I'm sure Bixby does. Check every drawer and cabinet. There's eighty-five hundred right there, so we're off to a good start."

"You know the dentist creeps me out, man," says Dante.

"You know we had no other choice. What happens when this guy disappears? People are gonna look for him. They're gonna come here and investigate," Damon says.

"You know how thorough the dentist is. He ain't gonna leave nothin'. They're gonna look for him, but nobody's ever gonna find anything," says Dante.

"Guys, can we think for a minute? That guy is dead over there. We already covered up a DUI that killed a young girl, now we're gonna cover this up? You're talking about a pro athlete that everyone knows. If he disappears, someone will eventually get to the bottom of what happened," says Dre.

"Well, he's got a knife in his back, bro. I don't know how much we can manipulate this," says Dante.

"He had alcohol on his breath," Joe says.

"Oh, yeah? Maybe we can use that," adds Damon.

"Dante, I don't know about this, bro. I know he was a client, but come on, Joe killed him in self-defense. We probably don't even hafta cover this up. Why not call the police and just tell them what happened?" Dre suggested.

"Dre, do you hear yourself? Reyes is all over us. He wants to end D & D. You think we could just report this? That man has a knife sticking out of his back. You're telling me they'll agree that this is self-defense? You don't really believe that. What's really goin' on with you, man? You seem a little off lately."

"I'm not off, Dante. I'm just sayin'...this is a big deal."

"Hell yeah, it's a big deal. I'm handling it though. I always handle it. The dentist is gonna come take him away. They're gonna clean up, and that's that."

"Okay, you're the boss. What about the girl?"

"We'll go see her today. Offer her a job. It'll be fine," Dante says calmly.

***

Roger's car zooms out of the private airplane hangar, headed toward the highway. He's exchanged the dim gleam of the street lamps in London for the bright lights of his city. Since he got back from Brazil, he hasn't had a chance to slow down and catch his breath. He begins to daydream about the first time he almost caught The Ghost.

It was a bright sunny day and Jim Stelton, a wealthy businessman from Chicago, was making an announcement that he was opening a headquarters in New York City. Roger knew Stelton was a target, so he had been following him throughout his time in New York, and thought he had the area secured. Halfway into the speech, Stelton took a shot to the head and went down behind the podium. Everyone began screaming and running. Roger just looked around, surveying everything. With all the chaos, he saw one woman casually walking away, and chased her. Her face was covered, and she was carrying what looked like a rifle case. After a long chase, he caught up to her and grabbed her. She pulled a knife from the side of the case and jammed it into Roger's gut.

SUSPECT BEHAVIOR

Of all the cases he's solved, The Ghost makes him feel like his career is incomplete. He's wanted to catch her for years. He begins to imagine chasing her for miles, finally catching up with her, and pulling the mask off her face. Before he can see her identity, he hears a loud horn. Roger snaps out of his daydream to see he's drifted into the lane of incoming traffic. He quickly swerves back into his lane. Struggling to catch his breath, he realizes he has to get it together.

***

At Bixby's house, there's a knock at the back door. Dante opens it and there stands the creepiest-looking old man Dre has ever seen. He has on an old trench coat and hat, with cold dead eyes. Standing behind him are two giant white guys, holding mops and buckets. The old man smiles and holds out the oldest hand, with the longest fingers he's ever seen.

"Mr. Sproles, I haven't seen you in a while. How are things?"

"You know, work can get a little messy sometimes."

"Thank goodness. If it didn't, I wouldn't have a job."

The old man laughs loudly while the giant men walk in and get to work. First, they put plastic down everywhere. Their next step is to put down a large plastic sheet and roll Bixby onto it. The men then remove the knife from his back. They tie it up and carry it out to their van, which is parked close to the back door. For the next couple of hours, they pick up every piece of wood and glass, and then mop all the floors. They spray the walls and wipe everything down.

"You have the money, my friend?" asks the old man.

"Of course. I have a question though. What do you usually do with the body?" asks Dante.

"We burn them and get rid of the ashes in the ocean, why?"

"I was hoping you could do something a little different."

134

"Different? Like what?"

"Well, he is famous, you know. I was thinking...he had been drinking...maybe..."

"Say no more, Mr. Sproles. I can arrange a crash. I'll make sure his car is incinerated."

"Thanks."

"Sure, it's gonna cost you twenty grand more, though."

"Dammit, Dentist! Fine. Come by the office tomorrow after hours."

"Death is expensive, you know."

"Yeah..."

***

Roger walks into Jay's computer room to see him in his pajamas and house shoes. He sits down and lets out a laugh.

"Whatchu laughin' at?" asks Jay.

"You have Batman pajamas on. Anyway, whatchu got for me?"

"Raj, that account is actually tied to a company."

"Really? What's the name of the company?"

"Raj, before I tell you that, let's talk."

"Jay, what's the name of the company?"

"This is the thing. I don't want you to jump to conclusions here. I know how bad you want The Ghost, but look. Man, this is the closest you've gotten. I don't want you to get tunnel vision and make a mistake. I need you around, bro."

"If you don't tell me the name of the company—"

"Are you hearing me, Raj?"

"I hear you, I really do."

"I hope so."

"So, what's the name of the company that the account was tied to?"

"Global Force Defense," Jay says with disappointment.

"What? What did you say?"

"Roger, it doesn't mean for sure that—"

"That's the company Cian works for. I was right."

"Raj, what if this is just coincidence?"

"She works for the company that has the account The Ghost gets paid from, and she was in the last two towns during the times there were assassinations. You know that's more than coincidence."

"All I'm saying is you need to be careful here. It may not be her."

"I'm always careful. I'm not gonna go to Global Defense, letting The Ghost know I'm onto her. I just hafta figure out my next step."

"I wish I could help you, Raj."

"You did help."

"Come on, bro. Take a break from this for a little while. Let me put my people on it."

"She's mine, Jay. Her days are numbered."

"I get that. Let me ask you a question. When is the last time you got eight hours of sleep?"

"Not since I got back."

"You're always preaching to me about the importance of rest. When I was playing, you never let up about it."

"I know, Jay, I know. I just don't have time for that now. I'm too close."

"You're not on top of your game, Raj. You look like you haven't slept in days."

"I haven't."

"Let me ask you, when's the last time you got some?"

Quashon Davis

"What?"

"You heard me. When's the last time you got some?"

"It's been a minute."

"What's a minute, Raj?"

"I don't know, maybe six months."

"Six months? So, you're tired as hell and you're carrying a loaded weapon around."

"Shut up."

"I'm just sayin', bro. This isn't the way to catch her. You know you're not at the top of your game right now. You know you need to be at your best."

"I'll get some rest, Jay. I just need to keep goin' for now."

"Raj, you're the best when you're at the top of your game. That's all I'm sayin'. Go down to the garage, bro. I know how much you like the classics. I got a sixty-three Cadillac convertible down there, firebird red. Why don't you take it out tonight, chill a little bit, then get some rest. You'll feel like a new man."

"A sixty-three?"

CHAPTER ELEVEN
ALL WOUND UP

"Good morning, last night around three am, police were called to exit 130 on the BQE, where a truck was on fire. It looked as if the driver took the exit too fast and lost control of his vehicle. The truck exploded after hitting the wall and had been burning for a while before first responders arrived on the scene. The vehicle was registered to New York Jets offensive lineman, Jack Bixby. Police verified that he was in the vehicle and is deceased. Once the fire was put out, the police confirmed that Bixby was in the vehicle and is deceased. There were no eyewitnesses, but police say the alcohol in the vehicle accelerated the flames. Jack Bixby was twenty-seven years old."

"Oh well, that guy was a prick," Dante says, watching it on the news.

"Yeah, he always was. I'm not even mad we barbequed his ass. The dentist is worth every penny," says Damon.

"Yeah, he is, but he creeps me out, bro."

"Yeah, he's creepy as hell. That's one thorough old guy though. Come on, the cops are probably tossing his place, and we're not even sweating."

"That's very true. I can't even lie."

"You talk to Jay yet about Raj helping us with Reyes?"

"Naw, I haven't heard from him yet. He'll call, though."

"I hope so. We gotta see what Ronnie found out."

"We will. Damon, we could have another problem."

"I can't deal with another one, Dante. What else?"

"Reyes visited R.J. at his house a while back."

"Oh, yeah? When did he tell you that?"

"He didn't. He never mentioned it."

"Damn, bro. You don't think he would sell us out?"

"I got somebody watching him. He may not say anything, but it's a little fishy that he never mentioned Reyes going by his house."

"Do you think Reyes only went to see him?"

"Whatchu mean, Damon?"

"What if he visited other people from the team?"

"Maybe I'm paranoid. Everyone seems to be a little funny, especially Dre. I don't know what's up with him. He's really been weird."

"We can't watch the whole team, boss. What should we do?"

"We don't have to. We just have to put some fail-safes in place. Everybody's got pressure points, Damon. You just hafta find out what they are. If the day ever comes that you need to, you squeeze."

"Start quietly nosing around. Get me something on Dre, Joe, and R.J."

"What about Ronnie?"

"Please, she would give her life before she sold out D & D."

"You ain't lying."

"So, get on it, big bro. We'll be fine. You know how we do. Always plan ahead, so you don't hafta worry."

"You got it."

"And, go get us some food."

***

Roger decides to take Jay's advice and leave the case alone for a little while. He calls Maya to see if she's available and once she tells him she is, he takes a long shower to try and wake himself up. His face is droopy, with bags under his eyes. He does the best he can and heads to pick her up. Roger may be able to take a break from the case, but his mind can't be shut off.

Did Cian really leave the country that day? Is Global Force knowingly working with The Ghost? If so, is she being contracted by our government? If she is, imagine how many countries would go to war with us.

An American assassin is murdering people from other countries on their home soil. This could be more of a mess than he realized. There's also the reality that if that's the case, he could be in a lot of danger. Plenty of people have contracted The Ghost and wouldn't want their business to ever get out.

Maya gets in the car looking great as always, with just a simple dress on.

"Hi, Raj, I'm glad you called."

"So am I. You hungry?"

"Not really. I could go for a shake, though."

"What? Is 'shake' code word for smoothie in healthy talk?"

"No, I want a milkshake. I've been eating good for a long time and I feel like kicking back a little today,"

"Finally, you're talking my language. How was your day?"

"It was good. I went to work, then I hit the gym. I came home and had some grilled chicken and asparagus."

"Well, that sounds just awful," laughs Roger.

"No, it was fantastic. If you knew what was in some of the food you eat, you wouldn't eat it."

"That's why I don't know."

"You're funny."

"You're not laughing."

"Don't start. I'm working on showing more emotion."

"You mean showing any emotion?"

"Yes, Raj."

"It's cool. I'm not here to give you a hard time."

"Is this your car? It's really nice."

"I wish. This is one of Jay's many cars."

"You okay? You look like you have a lot on your mind."

"I do. A case I'm working on is kinda rough."

"Oh, I'm sorry. You want to talk about it?"

"No, it's okay. I just wanna take a break from it, honestly."

"Well, in that case, today I had a patient that came in and they tried to pay for a tooth extraction with an EBT card."

"What?"

"I'm serious. They were poor and didn't have any dental insurance. The tooth was bothering him so much, he was desperate. He came in and offered me two hundred dollars' worth of food stamps."

"Wow, what did you do?"

"I took the tooth out for him. I didn't charge him, just made him wait 'til every patient was gone."

"That was really nice of you."

"Yeah, but I still made him get me two mango sorbets."

"Did you just make a joke?"

"No."

"Oh, I thought you were kidding."

"I was."

"You know, Maya, most people smile when they joke."

"I don't smile. You'll get used to it. I don't laugh or cry either."

"I noticed."

"Why does it bother you so much?"

"It's just hard to figure you out, that's all."

"I'm just like every other woman, Raj, I just don't show emotions."

"That sentence is an oxymoron."

Raj gets the milkshakes and drives up to a lookout point, facing all the lights of the city. They enjoy the view as well as the chunks of strawberry in their shakes.

"This view is amazing," Maya says, with her same straight face.

"Yeah, you can see the entire city from here."

"Raj, if you weren't a cop, what would you have been?"

"Well, the plan wasn't for me to be a cop, growing up. I wanted to play professional football. I just knew I was gonna make it. I was a standout athlete in high school, and got a full scholarship to the University of Michigan. While I was playing, I broke my leg on a freak play. The doctors said I couldn't play anymore."

"That must've been difficult."

"Very. Up until that point, it was the only thing I knew. It was the only thing I was good at. I broke my leg, tore my ACL, MCL, and my meniscus. It was really bad."

"Oh, my God. How bad did it hurt?"

"Hurt? I passed out. It was the worst pain I ever felt."

"I can't imagine. Well, let's not talk about that. Do you miss Brazil?"

"Not at all. I'm glad I'm back home. There was an incident here and I was forced to leave. It's a long story, but it got sorted out."

"Well, we seem to have plenty of time."

"My wife was cheating on me. I shot the wrong guy."

"What? Did you kill him?"

"Of course not. I left before they could arrest me."

"Did you ever find out who your wife was cheating on you with?"

"Yeah, I did."

"Wait a minute, how are you here now?"

"I was pardoned."

"Pardoned? By who?"

"The president."

"Of the United States? Why?"

"They needed me on this case I'm working on."

"You are interesting. Roger Merrit, man of mystery and intrigue."

"Not hardly. I'm just a guy."

"If you say so."

"Okay, you're granted three wishes, what are they?" he asks.

"Hmmmm, A billion dollars."

"Of course."

"I wish guns were never invented."

"That's an interesting one."

"Last, I wish I could go back and change what my father did."

"Sorry?"

"It's okay. I have to live with it. He took my mom and all my emotions at one time."

"Well, you're still a great person."

"You really think so?"

"I wouldn't be here if I didn't."

"So, are you gonna kiss me or what? You can't tell by my face, I'm ready?" she asks.

Roger looks in her face to see the same serious expression she always has.

"I just made a joke, Raj."

"Wow, you're coming around," he says, leaning in to kiss her.

They begin as small pecks on the lips, until Maya opens wide and wrestles Roger's tongue to the floor of his mouth. The two kiss passionately over the lights of the city. Although Maya still has her same serious look, he is finally able to read her eyes. Roger lifts her from her seat and places her on his lap in a straddle position as the kissing continues. The show of strength titillates her as she lets out a gasp. Maya can feel all the manhood that Roger is blessed with underneath her. She pulls her breasts over the top of her dress and lets them dangle inches from his face. He engulfs her healthy nipples one at a time into his watery mouth. Maya moans softly as everything inside of her is pulsating.

Roger has only had two partners in his life. One was his mate of twenty-one years, the other he dated for three years in Brazil. Because of this, he only knows one way to make love, to give it everything he has. Before she can recover from the war his mouth waged on her breasts, Roger lifts her from his lap and places her legs on his shoulders, resting her back against the steering wheel. As Roger's face probes the inside of Maya's dress, she is high in the air with a full view of the city lights. He finds his mark, licking and sucking, and gently pulling. Maya's body is throbbing and tingling in ways she's never felt before. She reaches down and unzips his pants, quickly using the opening in his underwear to expose his thickness. Roger's tongue has run across her spot several times, her body stiffening with each encounter. Her view of the city goes blurry as Maya explodes, letting out a loud scream, surprising and confusing herself.

Before she can regain her senses, Roger's shaft has penetrated her moist inlet. She slowly moves up and down, while they remain eye to eye amid the sweat of the dry summer heat. Maya tries to look at the stars to take her mind off the depths Roger is reaching, but the handsome face drenched in sweat can't be ignored. The sight of her perfectly round breasts and hard nipples bouncing in front of him keeps him solid and eager. She begins to move faster on him. Finally, she gets up and turns her back to him, places her hands at the top of the windshield of the convertible, and slowly slides down on him again. Her eyes widen as from behind, it feels like she's starting all over again. Roger can feel every inch of himself claiming her precious territory slowly. Once adjusted, she speeds up rapidly. He lifts her dress to see her muscular shape working. Maya's eyes close as she once again feels the rush of a climax coming on. She yells loudly as her juices cascade down Roger like an erupting volcano. The visual causes him to feel the familiar tingle on his left side. Roger holds Maya tightly as he explodes, sending every ounce of energy he has into her. The two instantly fall asleep and don't move until 5:00 am.

***

TLPSA is a very unique private institution. Instead of a traditional summer break, they only have off the month of August. With only days before their brief summer break, the students do everything they can to take advantage of all the amenities they have. The singers take up every singing area, every microphone, and every voice instructor's spare moments. The dancers practice throughout the day, utilizing the stages and instructors as much as possible. At this school, most of the students don't want to take a vacation. They're aspiring singers, dancers, or some other type of artist, whose parents pay the hefty tuition so they can make it. In a dark corner of the school in a small room, James is playing the piano. At the age of four, he could easily play in front of a large crowd and not miss a beat. He also has a golden voice. James loves watching old videos of his dad playing basketball, but he has no interest in sports yet. It's still early, but the fact that he can sing and play the piano as well as he can, probably means he won't change. He begins to sing, his eyes closed as he concentrates, hitting every note.

The door opens and Ted peeks his head in. He disappears and Sapphire walks in. She stands and watches James play the piano singing for a couple of minutes. She is still blown away by the fact that he's her son. He is everything she always imagined her child would be. His talent level for his age is unbelievable. He stops playing and she applauds, causing him to turn around.

"Sapphire, you're back," he says, getting up to hug her.

"I am. How are you today?"

"Good, I got chocolate chip cookies."

"You do? Are we sharing?"

"Yes, I have four. You can have one."

"Yay, you're so generous. You excited about your vacation?"

"Yes. My mommy and daddy are taking me to Disneyworld."

"Oh really? That sounds nice. Can I go?"

"Yes."

"You're sweet. James, can I ask you something?"

"Yes."

"Do you love your mommy?"

"Yes."

"Why?"

"Cause she's my mommy. She makes me food, and she plays with me. She sings with me, even though Mommy can't sing. She makes me cookies when I'm sick, and we go to the park a lot. We have food fights. She takes me to the movies every time I want to see something."

Sapphire's eyes are welling up with tears. She tries to fight them off, but she's failing. She tells James she has to go and rushes out the door. By the time she gets to her car, she's full-on crying. Luckily, the enchantress of R & B has fully tinted windows. She tries to calm down. Once she does, she calls Jay.

"Hello?"

"I hate you."

"Hello, Sapphire."

"You turned my own son against me. You're a monster."

"What are you talkin' about now?"

"He thinks that bitch of yours is some hero or something. It's not right."

"That's the only mother he knows. Of course she's a hero to him."

"He's *my* son, I should be his hero."

"I told you I was sorry. What else do you want me to do?"

"You can shove that sorry up your entitled ass. The world is about to learn what kind of monster you are. What are you gonna do then?"

"After you do that, what's gonna happen? Are you gonna magically become his hero?"

"I will over time."

"Right...over time you'll be the woman that took him from his family. You think that's gonna win the kid over? When he doesn't see us anymore, but he's stuck in the house with no one because you're on tour. You really think that's better for him?"

"To hell with you. He's my son, mine. You don't get to dictate what I do."

"Okay, no problem, Sapphire. What would you like me to do?"

"Can the polite act, Jay. You got all these people fooled, not me. I know what you are. Soon, everyone else is gonna know too."

"And then what? You ride off into the sunset? James just starts calling you Mommy?"

She hangs up on him. Frustrated, Jay throws his phone at the wall, destroying it.

CHAPTER TWELVE
THE CONTINGENCY MASTER

R EYES SITS IN HIS OFFICE, poring over files he has on various D & D clients. Every trail has gone cold, and he's not sure what his next step is going to be. The Derrick Fair angle was a dead-end. The Tina Powell situation was explained away. Every time he gets close, they have an answer. Frustrated, he considers letting his phone ring, but decides to answer.

"Reyes."

"This is R.J. from D & D."

"It's about damn time. You ready to talk?"

"I want total immunity."

"Of course, of course, how fast can you get here?"

"I'll meet with you tomorrow afternoon."

"Great. Anything you want to tell me in the meantime? You know, just to hold me over?"

"No man. I'll see you tomorrow."

Reyes has a wide smile on his face the Kool-Aid man would be jealous of. He's tempted to do a little dance, but decides not to. As he begins to clear his desk, his phone rings again.

"Reyes."

"This is Andre, you bastard. I want to talk."

"I'm sure you do. I'm glad you came to your senses. Breakfast tomorrow?"

"Yeah, a'ight."

"Good, meet me at nine am at Sharky's."

"Fine."

Once Dre hangs up, his phone is ringing. He sees it's Dante. Nervous, he immediately looks around to see if he was being watched. After surveying the area, he nervously answers.

"Hey, Dante, what's up?"

"Hey, bro, emergency meeting in one hour at headquarters."

"Okay. I'll be there," Dre says nervously.

He makes his way over to D & D headquarters slowly. With all the mess they have going on, what could this meeting be about? Did someone see them at Bixby's house? The nerves in the pit of his stomach are going crazy.

***

Joe has been doing a lot of thinking since Bixby's death. He feels bad, but he doesn't want to go to jail. A lot of hard drinking isn't making him feel any better. He just got the call for the emergency meeting. He's thinking it has something to do with Bixby.

***

R.J. arrives last at D & D wondering what's going on. He takes the elevator up and walks out into the office. He greets everyone on his way to the conference room. He is also confused. When he walks in, Joe, Dre, Ronnie, and Damon are sitting down. He takes a seat and Dante walks in. He drops folders in front of everyone, telling them not to open them.

150

Quashon Davis

"Sorry to drag you guys in here like this, but it couldn't be helped. Almost fifteen years ago, Damon and I were living on the streets. We were robbing people every day, just so we could eat. It looked like we were gonna end up dead or in jail. One day, we went to rob a guy and saw that it was our guy from the Big Brother program, Jay Jones. He talked to us about getting off the streets, going through college, and doin' something. It was the same crap we'd heard a thousand times, but it was coming from a guy we had mad respect for. We told him we couldn't afford to go to school, but he said there's plenty of ways to do it. He gave us some money, talked to us, and by the time he walked away, we were in a different mindset."

Dante pauses for a moment and looks out the window.

"Before you knew it, we both took out student loans and got degrees in sports management and medicine. Jay was our first client. After his first season, we banked ten million from his hundred-million-dollar contract, and another five from his shoe deal. Next thing you know, we had twenty clients. One of them was a ball player with ten kids, and eight baby mommas. We'll call him, 'number thirty-three.' He got a woman pregnant that was a known gold digger when it came to athletes. She had three kids from three athletes in three different sports, and this idiot got her pregnant with her fourth, and his eleventh. He didn't want his wife to find out, so he came to us. We figured since he was a client of ours, we'd try to help him out."

He reaches for a bottle of water at the center of the table, opening it and taking several sips.

"I wanted to push her down a flight of stairs, Damon wanted to put her on a plane to Haiti and have someone snatch her passport when she landed. I won't tell you whose idea we settled on, but I will say we fixed our client's situation. That was the first time. Word spread among athletes. Next thing you know, we had two hundred clients. We were fixing all types of situations. Me and Damon bought a yacht. We never looked back. We built this company from one client, to an empire.

Even though we have a lot of employees, you're the ones that do the dirty work. The rest of the people in this building don't know the things we do. I appreciate you guys. I think of you all as family. That's why I want you all to know this isn't personal at all. But, you need to understand, this thing we built here, I will protect at all costs. Go ahead, open your folders. I know that Reyes met with each of you. We worked too hard to destroy this. In your folders, you'll each find specific incentives not to talk to Reyes."

R.J. opens his envelope to find pictures of his father in prison, photos of him eating, working out, even showering. There's also a schedule, showing the times throughout the day that he's in every area of the prison.

"Are you threatening my father's life?" R.J. asks, standing up.

"Of course not. I don't make threats. I don't have to. Like I said, it's not personal at all."

R.J. sits back down frustrated, staring at the pictures of his father in prison. The only person in the world he cares about is his dad. He knows Dante has him.

Joe opens his envelope to see several pictures. The first two are of his young daughters. The next one shows him in his car, sniffing cocaine. The final two pictures show him in his bloody clothes the day he killed Bixby. Underneath all of the pictures is a copy of a motion he recently filed in court for visitation rights. He nods his head to show he's beaten.

"Well, you got me by the balls. Consider me quiet," he says.

Dre opens his envelope and takes a deep breath. There are pictures of his car at the spot where Derrick Fair and Tina Powell's accident happened. He immediately realizes what happened. When he called them from Derrick's car and told them to come and get his, they took pictures first. There are shots of his car parked with broken lights from both cars on the ground around it. Dre knows there would be nothing he could say if this got out.

"Damn you, Dante," he says.

"Damn *me*? I hired each one of you myself. You were broke when you walked into my office the first time. You make six figures now. All of you do. You make your own hours. You're in the office twice a week for a few hours. I give y'all bonuses, unlimited vacations, access to the jet. Why would any of you not tell me Reyes is stalking you? Loyalty is everything. Ronnie, aren't you gonna open your envelope?"

"No."

"Why not?"

"Cause I know it's empty. It damn well better be empty," she says.

Dante and Damon laugh hysterically.

"You know me too well, girl. You're all dismissed. From this day forward, any of you that have an issue with Reyes, just have him call me," he says.

Damon and Dante walk out of the conference room, leaving everyone else sitting there. R.J., Joe, and Dre are still stunned by what just happened. They just continue looking at the pictures they received.

"He shoulda fired all three of you, and kicked your asses," Ronnie says, getting up and leaving the room.

R.J. and Dre look over at each other before taking out their phones. They both send text messages to Reyes, telling him their meetings are off.

***

Roger has spent the last couple of hours on the computer, looking up everything he can find on The Ghost's last few victims. His thought is that if each of them handled the drive, he can figure out who the next victim is. He has too many unanswered questions. Everything keeps leading into dead--ends. Luckily for him, his evening with Maya helped to clear his head.

"Alves had the drive, The Ghost killed Alves. I get it. Alves showed the drive to Markos, The Ghost killed Markos. Markos met with Benjamin at his home. They were watching him. They assumed he shared whatever was on that drive with him, so The Ghost killed Benjamin. I know The Ghost isn't finished yet. Why though? The Ghost recovered the disk drive from Markos. What am I missing? If The Ghost is still here, why is she? Alves knew he was in trouble the moment he stole that drive. Markos told Benjamin he was in danger when he saw what was on the drive. Wait a minute, Alves knew he was in trouble the moment he stole the drive. If I knew I was in trouble, what would I have done first? Hell, the first thing I would've done is…of course. Alves made a copy of the drive. He sold the copy and kept the original. The Ghost hasn't found it!"

Within seconds, Roger is speeding toward Alves' home. He already knows what to expect, thanks to years of detective work. It's time to find a needle in a haystack. Alves lived in a hole-in-the-wall apartment in the Bronx Projects. He makes his way through the courtyard, rushing by the local thugs that are all standing around, smoking and talking. They all look him up and down, but Roger's massive stature keeps anyone from wanting to try him. Alves lived on the tenth floor. Roger decides to take the stairs, rather than take his chances in the hood elevator. He quickly picks the lock on apartment 1011 and walks in. His intuition was right. The apartment has already been ransacked. There's crap everywhere.

He begins his thorough search. There's a reason he's one of the best at what he does. Clearly, this apartment was searched by more than one agency already. For the next two hours, Roger searches every inch of the apartment. He laughs as he finds drugs everywhere that the cops and whatever other agencies missed when they looked. He opens the bedroom closet and goes through all the clothes, every coat pocket, inner lining, and the walls. He doesn't find anything. Above the clothing is an exclusive sneaker collection, all Jordan's.

"Impressive," he says to himself.

He checks every sneaker, but when he gets to the last pair, they're covered in mud and dog crap. Roger puts on an extra pair of gloves and takes one out of the closet. After pulling the laces out of the shoe, he shoves his hand inside and near the toe, he feels something. He pulls out a small drive and smiles.

"Of course, he made a copy."

Roger puts it in his pocket and leaves the apartment. He knows he can't go to the precinct or to Jay's house to see what's on the drive. Whatever it is has caused everyone who's seen it to be killed. He gets in his car, knowing he has to think carefully about where he checks the drive from.

***

Dre's car pulls in front of Dawn's house. He's playing some R & B, trying to clear his head, still recovering from the shocking meeting he just had at D & D. His head is swimming with emotions. He's scared, confused, angry and worst of all, vulnerable. He's so nervous that he can't even take a breath to figure out what to do next. The one thing Dre is sure of is that he doesn't want to be alone. Dawn comes out of the house and gets in his car, kissing him.

"Dre, are you okay?"

"Not really."

"What's going on?"

"I can't really get into it. It's some work stuff, that's all."

"Every time you're stressing, you won't talk about it. I can tell there's things you want to tell me. I keep telling you that you can tell me anything. Why won't you talk to me, Dre?"

155

"There's some things that I just can't get into."

"Dre, do you know why we haven't had sex yet?"

"I didn't really think about it."

"I like you a lot. But, I can't give you all of me, until I know you're giving me all of you. That can't happen until you stop hiding everything from me. I can't trust you. I know you're a good guy, but I don't know who you are. Why can't you show me?"

"You won't like who I really am."

"Why can't you let me be the judge of that? I like who I've known up to this point. You know you can be yourself with me. Just talk—"

"One day, Dawn. One day."

"Today should be that day, Dre. I don't care what you do, just who you are. As long as that doesn't change, we're good."

"These last few weeks were something I really needed. I don't want to lose you."

"You won't lose me, Dre," she says, kissing him. She takes his hand and places it on her leg, then steadily moves it up. "I'm tired of holding back, Dre, I know you are too."

He takes a deep breath and fights back a tear from coming down his face.

"I met your cousin. Tina was in an accident with one of our clients. I was there. I paid her and told her she couldn't tell anyone about it. The first thing she told me was call 911. I told her if we did that, I couldn't hook her up. I gave her some money and she was on her way. She didn't know she had a blood vessel that burst in her brain. It's my fault she's gone. It's my fault. My company is very good at what they do. We didn't leave anything. I'm sorry, Dawn. I'm so sorry."

"I forgive you."

"You what?"

"I forgive you."

Quashon Davis

"Why would you forgive me, Dawn?"

"Because you finally 'fessed up."

"What do you mean?"

Dawn makes a fist and speaks into it, "Move in, we got him."

Two police cars quickly move in on them. Dre looks over at Dawn, confused.

"You were on the job this whole time?"

"Yes. It took you long enough to talk. I thought I was gonna hafta give you some to get you to speak up. You have the right to remain silent. Anything you say can and will be used against you in the court of law. You have the right to an attorney. If you can't afford an attorney, one will be appointed to you. Do you understand the rights I just read to you?"

"You played me. I can't believe you played me like this."

"I did my job. One day, you'll realize that. The same way you were doing your job when you covered up that poor girl's murder."

"She's not even your cousin, is she?"

"No, of course not."

"You're good. I really thought you liked me."

"Liked you? Please. You know the name, Andrea Hawkins?"

"Sounds familiar, should I?"

"She was raped by three college football players not too long ago. Your company covered it up to protect them. She's my niece. When Reyes told me what he wanted to do, I was the first to volunteer."

The police take Dre out of the car and handcuff him. Dawn takes him over to the police car and guides him in.

"Just so you know, I only date white boys," she says as she shuts the door.

157

Reyes walks up and smiles at him from the sidewalk.

"There is a God, Andre. I'm thanking him for not having to give you immunity. We're about to go shut them down permanently. I owe it all to you, my friend. Take him away, boys."

"Reyes, wait. How long have you been trying to bring D & D down?" asks Dre.

"Too long, why?"

"Maybe you should call Dante first and tell him you're coming to get him."

"Why would I do that?"

"Before you take half your precinct there, you might wanna talk to him first."

For a long time, Reyes stares at Dre sitting in the car, trying to figure out what exactly he should do.

"Are you really listening to this idiot? He knows he's going to jail, just take him away," Dawn says.

"I'm your superior, not the other way around. Go wait in the car for now."

Dawn walks away, pissed. Reyes takes out his phone and dials Dante.

"Yeah?"

"The almighty Dante Sproles. I'm sure you know who this is."

"Of course. I figured you'd be calling me sooner or later. What can I do for you?"

"Your boy, Dre, just told an undercover what really happened the night of Tina Powell's murder. I'm having arrest warrants drawn up for you and your team, and search warrants for your property also. D & D is finished."

"Wow, really?"

"Yeah, really. I'll see you soon."

Quashon Davis

"Reyes, before you go can I say something?"

"What?"

"You're a widower, right?"

"Watch it, Sproles. You better be very careful with the next words that come out of your mouth."

"Your son...his name is Luis, right?"

"So, what?"

"He's in his second year at USC, I believe."

"Why are you into my business like this?"

"For times like this, my friend. Tuition per year at USC is fifty-four thousand dollars. Health insurance is nineteen hundred a year. Room and board is fifteen thousand a year. Once you tack on books, personal expenses, and transportation, you're lookin' at about seventy-three thousand bucks a year."

"What's your point?"

"My point is that neither you nor your son took out a student loan. On top of that, he's current."

"I...um...I don't see where this is going."

"You currently pay twenty-three thousand a year in rent, three hundred a month for your car, and your phone and other bills are about six hundred bucks. You make about eighty grand a year, yet you're paying out around a hundred and thirty grand. How are you doing that, Reyes?"

"You dare try to threaten a cop with your nonsense? You don't have anything on me. I have everything on you."

"You've been after me a long time, Reyes. You know I'm always a step ahead of you. You can try to execute a warrant if you like, but you would be quite busy explaining to Internal Affairs how you're paying for all that stuff. I'll leave it at that. Whoever's pocket you're in doesn't matter to me. I know you want young Luis to stay in school. Besides, you're living way beyond your means, my friend. You may wanna let this go. If they start lookin', you would be in major trouble. Listen, I gotta go, but you may wanna let Dre off. I'm sure you can come up with a reason. You're a smart guy, except when you go against me," he says, hanging up.

Reyes stands on the sidewalk, shaking from the stress of his interaction with Dante. He finally has what he's been after for years, evidence that would bring down D & D and put them in prison. He's spent hundreds of sleepless nights chasing down leads and shaking down potential witnesses in an effort to end them. He's so close he can taste it, the accolades, the satisfaction, even the promotion. As much as he wants all of that, Reyes has been on the take for years. He would never be able to pay for his son's college otherwise. He closes his eyes and takes several deep breaths. Dawn gets out of the car and stomps over to him, visibly upset.

"If you don't prosecute them, I will," she blasts.

"You won't do anything except follow my instructions."

"What happened, Reyes? You've been trying to get them forever. What did they say to you?"

"Release the prisoner," he says.

"What? Why the hell are you doing this? What's going on?"

"We didn't have the proper paperwork filed for this undercover operation. Because of that, any information we obtained isn't useable," says Reyes.

"I listen to you bitch every day about how D & D gets good people to look the other way. After all of this, you're just another one on the list."

"I've learned that's not actually what they do. They prove over and over that there aren't any good people left. Let him go."

"Oh, my God!" Dawn blasts, taking Dre out of the cop car and un-cuffing him.

Quashon Davis

"It's never too late to come home, *sister*," Dre says sarcastically.

"You're free to go," says Reyes.

"Sorry, man. I know what you're going through, though," Dre tells him.

"I know you do, Andre. I know you do."

***

Jay is driving home from his private gym. A strenuous, high-intensity, boxing training session wasn't enough to get his mind off of all the stress he's experiencing. Recently, his blood pressure has shot up. He's experiencing headaches, and constant stomach issues. Whenever he's driving, he always sees at least one person with his old jersey on. Even through his dark black tinted windows, his fans always seem to know it's him. They wave from the streets when he goes by, and kids chase the car down streets. Once in a while, he'll pull over and sign autographs, take pictures, and talk to fans. They can never get enough of him. He can't imagine what's going to happen when all that attention goes away. People are going to hate him. Worse than that, his own wife will probably hate him also. The #MeToo Movement has shown him how quickly a man's reputation can be destroyed. He keeps checking Google and CNN to see if she's told the public yet.

"Call Roger," he says.

"Jay, what's going on, bro?"

"Man, I'm really stressing. I don't know what to do."

"Stressing over things you can't control is only gonna hurt you. You taught me that."

"I can't help it, Raj. I can't think of a way out."

"For once, there may not be a way out. You may hafta lose on this one."

"If Shel finds out, she'll be crushed."

161

"That's true. Man, that's gonna be rough."

"You're not helping, Raj."

"Sorry, bro, I can't lie. You're in a rough spot. I wouldn't wanna be you right now. The good thing is, you've been in rough spots your whole life. You've seen all kinds of adversity. I was there when you got shot, remember? We were kids. That summer league we were playing in was just a summer thing to do. You were set to go star at Duke. They told you your basketball career was over. You didn't sit around feeling sorry for yourself. You worked your butt off and not only made it to the league; you were one of the best ever. Come on, man, you know you'll get through it."

"Raj, my name is everything to me. Even at my lowest points, people would see me and give me respect. I can't lose that."

"You already have, man. You should tell Shel before she sees it on the news or social media. Let her hear it from you. She's gonna be pissed. I can't lie, she might leave you. For some reason, it means something if they hear it from you and not someone else."

"I can't tell her."

"Man, you still actin' like you got a choice."

"Damn, man. This really sucks."

"I know. I wish I could do something, man."

"Well, whatever. What are you up to?"

"Well, The Ghost has basically been contracted to kill anyone that saw the information on a drive. I backtracked all of her victims and found a copy of it."

"Are you serious? What the hell is on it?"

"I haven't looked yet."

"Why?"

Quashon Davis

"Think about it, Jay. If everyone who's seen what's on it has been killed, and The Ghost charges eight million a kill, what does that tell you?"

"Uh, I don't know..."

"It tells me that there's some major players behind this. Not only that, the moment you boot up that drive, they're tracking the signal and sending The Ghost."

"Okay, so what are you gonna do?"

"I'm gonna set a trap for The Ghost."

"Oh, God..."

"I'll be careful, Jay. I promise."

"Raj, you're my best friend, you know that. I trust you with everything. I just don't want you to mess with this woman anymore."

"I got this, bro. I'm ending this once and for all. You gotta believe in me."

"Okay, Raj, get her then."

"I am. Listen, if anything goes wrong, I've got a few things I need you to do for me."

"Anything, you know that."

CHAPTER THIRTEEN
A TRAP FIT FOR A GHOST

ROGER WALKS UP TO A large warehouse on the Lower East Side and picks the lock. He turns on a single light and surveys the room, carefully learning the area around him. Ignoring his phone ringing, he takes hours looking over every inch of the room, until he feels he's ready. Roger has carefully planned for every move The Ghost can make. He walks to the big open space in the back of the warehouse and opens his laptop. Once it's on, he inputs the drive and boots it up. After a minute of loading, he hears a conversation between the vice president of the United States and a Russian. They discuss some U.S. secrets, regarding defense and infrastructure. The V.P. then offers up the president's schedule of where he'll be and when for the month of September.

Oh God, it's worse than I thought, Roger thinks. *Not only did the vice president tell some of our country's secrets to a Russian, he offered up the president on a platter. He's clearly trying to have him assassinated. The Russians are willing to make that happen in exchange for secrets and information. It's obvious why anyone that's seen this has been killed.*

Roger quickly hides in the warehouse and makes sure his gun is loaded, with the safety off. He waits patiently for The Ghost to arrive. He's waited a long time for this moment. He's trying to focus, but the thoughts of what this means are creeping into his mind. The one case he was never able to close. He's often daydreamed about the day he would stroll into the precinct with The Ghost in cuffs. After she killed the kid, Roger never gave up. Even during his time in Brazil, he tracked her assassinations on the Internet, making notes and keeping a folder on her. The Midtown Rapist, The Sniper, The Night Hacker, The Info Thief, Roger has caught them all. Regardless of his heroics, he sits in this dark warehouse, awaiting his career-defining moment.

This is for all the people that told me she couldn't be caught. This will be in the face of everyone that told me to let it go or she'd kill me. She needs to pay for all the lives she's ruined, including mine.

His obsession with her ends tonight. It wasn't a long wait. Within fifteen minutes, he hears a low creak on the floor, followed by another one. From his hiding spot in the corner, he sees a dark figure drop down from a window near the ceiling. The Ghost lands quietly and begins looking around. She pulls out her knife and sneaks across the floor, checking out the area. Roger is crouched in his hiding spot, not making a sound. After waiting for years, he has plenty of patience. He watches her survey the room for several minutes. She doesn't notice Roger in the corner surrounded by trash and old boxes. He has his gun aimed directly at her head. He is struggling with the urge to shoot the assassin. Despite her long list of victims, there's only one he's concerned with, Fritz Goeth, Jr. A face he sees every day. A young child's life was cut short because of The Ghost's precious identity. The masked figure looks in both directions, before noticing the laptop. She slowly makes her way over to it when Roger jumps out of his hiding spot.

"Freeze. Turn around slowly," he demands.

The shadowy figure turns around and Roger stares into the face of the dark-masked assailant. He cocks his gun, trying to decide if he should just kill her.

"Get on your knees now," he shouts.

She gets on her knees and places her hands on her head. Roger walks up, but stays ten feet away. He learned from his last mistake.

"Slowly take the mask off," he orders.

"I can't do that," she whispers.

"Take it off or I'll shoot you and do it myself."

She removes the mask and Roger isn't surprised at all. He looks at Cian with a feeling of pride. He was right. He said it was her and there she is. As he prepares to cuff her, something he said in the past is on his mind.

Nothing The Ghost does is random.

He takes a look around before walking up to her. As soon as he takes a step, there's a loud popping sound, and he feels searing heat in his back. Roger falls to the ground and rolls around. When he manages to sit up he looks down, seeing the blood rushing from his body in several places. He immediately knows the miscalculation he made. He looks up and sees another masked person walk up to Cian, then another, and another. They remove their masks and there they are. It's Maya, Tess, and Angie. They help Cian up and all stare at Roger.

"Of course. It had to be all of you. It's the only way The Ghost can cover so much ground. Y-you charge eight million a kill and split it four ways. You're the one that put the gym flyer on my car to get me to go there and meet you. God, I blew it..." Roger says, coughing up blood.

"You should've just let this go, Roger," says Cian.

"No, I shouldn't have. You all need to pay for all the lives you took. What about Fritz Goeth, Jr., that child you killed? Where's his justice?"

"He saw my face. We didn't have a choice," Angie says.

"There's always a choice," Roger says, while continuing to cough up blood.

Quashon Davis

"You're good, Roger, but we're The Ghost for a reason. The moment you got that pardon, we had our eyes on you. You plan ahead, we plan backwards and work our way ahead. I wish it could've been different. I'm outta here, this is sad," Cian says.

As the girls quickly file out, Maya stays and stands in front of Roger. They stare at each other for several seconds as she watches the life exiting his body. From the corner of her eye a tear forms and rolls down her face, followed by a wrinkle in the corner of her cheek that almost resembles a smile.

"Thanks for that. I knew you would have a great smile," Roger whispers.

"I'm sorry, Roger. I was just gonna keep an eye on you, but you got too close. I didn't want to hurt you."

"I know you didn't. You had a job to do, and I had a job to do. In another life, it could've been different."

"I would've liked that," she says as her face is full of sadness.

"You didn't win, you know."

"It's not a competition, Roger."

"For me it was. I-I always need to win..." he says as he takes his last breath.

Maya takes a dusty old blanket from a box in the corner of the warehouse and covers Roger's body. She stands in front of him for a minute, mumbling something to herself before going over to the laptop and taking the thumb drive from it. She looks back one last time before quickly putting her mask back on and exiting through the window.

"Actually, *we* never lose, Roger," she whispers on her way out.

***

SUSPECT BEHAVIOR

The long motorcade makes its way into the cemetery. There's hundreds of police there in full uniform. The cars all stop in the middle of the grounds. Jay and Train, along with four other men, carry the dark gray casket shrouded with the American flag to its final destination. They place it down and an officer removes the flag and folds it into a triangle. He then walks it over to Miesha and hands it to her. Her face is full of tears as she sits with Marie, facing the casket. The line of officers fire off their rifles into the air. Miesha can't stop thinking about the conversation they had. She called him back when he was in the warehouse, but Roger didn't answer. She never got to tell him how she really felt and now, she never will.

Jay stands, staring at the casket in stunned silence. Even with shades on, it's clear that he's crying heavily. Jay has gone over it in his mind several times, wondering what he could've done differently. His best friend is gone. After the preacher says a few words, he announces that Jay will be delivering the eulogy. He adjusts his shades and takes a deep breath, before addressing everyone.

"Good afternoon, everyone, Roger Merrit was my best friend. In a non-trusting world, he was the only person I trusted with my life. We met when we were young kids. I loved basketball, he loved football. We told each other everything. We were inseparable. We celebrated great times, and we were there for each other during bad times. Those of you that worked with him knew he was a genius. He's one of the best detectives that ever lived. What many of you didn't know was that he read a book a week for about twenty years. No matter how bad things were going for him, the first thing he would always ask you was, 'How are things going with you?' He always put himself last. He worked hard, and he loved hard too. Roger only loved one woman in all the years that I knew him. He would've moved the Earth for her."

Quashon Davis

Jay's voice trembles as he takes a slow but shaky deep breath to center himself before continuing.

"But honestly, he was the type of guy that if he knew you, he would do anything for you. A guy that was a fugitive from most of the people here for years and not one of you has a bad thing to say about him. Look at how many people are here paying their respects. I remember when he had to flee the country. He said to me, 'Jay, when you're a hero to everyone, eventually a situation will come along that makes you become the villain.' I'm proud to say, I love Roger Merrit. He's gonna live on. We'll tell his stories to our kids and they'll pass them onto theirs. You know, I keep asking myself, what could I have done differently to keep my best friend alive? The thing is, he lived the way he wanted to, and he died doing what he loved. Even though we'll miss him terribly, I know he doesn't have any regrets. I know he's looking down on us and he's saying, 'I can't believe Captain Rayton is here.' "

Everyone erupts with laughter.

"But seriously, I hope you all know how fantastic this man was. When The Midtown Rapist was terrorizing our streets at night, Roger caught him. When The Sniper had everyone afraid to go outside, Roger brought him to justice. The mayor gave him the key to the city. He wasn't just my hero, he was everyone's hero. I'll miss our late-night talks, our trips to R & B's, and our competitions. My best friend is gone, but I'm gonna live on as he would want me to. I'm gonna honor him as best I can. We all lost a hero today and I lost a brother. Thank you, everyone."

As Roger's casket is lowered into the ground amid a sea of sadness, Maya's standing in the corner by herself, watching with her usual serious look. She takes her shades off and stares at the gravesite.

Miesha is sobbing inconsolably, her eyes full of tears. She can't seem to accept what's going on.

"Are you okay?" asks Marie.

"No, I'm not okay."

"I understand. Is there anything I can do?"

"I think it's time you moved out."

"What?"

"Marie, I think you should leave the house."

"Why? Because of this?"

"No, because it's not working. It hasn't for a long time."

"You're just upset about Roger. I get it."

"It has nothing to do with that. The writing's been on the wall for a while."

"That's what you really want?"

"Yes."

"Fine." Marie gets up and walks away from her, heading toward the cars.

Captain Rayton is shaking hands and speaking to people. Eventually, he makes it up to Jay.

"Mr. Jones, I'm really sorry about Roger. He was a great detective."

"He would've loved to have heard you say that."

"He knew I felt that way. He was brilliant. I'm just old school, you know? We butted heads a lot. I respected the hell out of him, though."

"I appreciate that, Captain. I'm sure he does too."

Pete is standing off to the side, looking as if he's lost his best friend. He and Roger went back quite a ways. They had some rocky times, but Pete genuinely loved the guy. He stands there, looking at the grave in disbelief.

Reyes looks like a beaten man. After the situation with D & D, he hasn't been the same. He's been drinking and staying awake night after night. Depression is all over his face. After that fiasco, he was lucky to come out with his job intact, after backing off from charging D & D, claiming he made a mistake.

Reyes, what's goin' on, man?" Jay asks, shaking his hand.

"I'm just trying to get by. Sorry about Roger. He was a great detective. I had the utmost respect for him."

"I appreciate that, Reyes. I really do. You know, he gave me something to give you in case anything happened to him."

"He did?"

"Yeah he did," Jay says, handing him an envelope.

Reyes opens the envelope that says, "The Ghost" on it, and looks at the pictures and information inside. The beaten look on his face perks up. He quickly thumbs through them and lights up.

"It's all his notes," he says, while turning the pages.

Reyes' phone rings and he speaks to someone briefly. With all the cops at the funeral, it was impossible to get ahold of anyone at the station. He gets off the phone and frowns.

"What's up, Reyes?"

"I can never get time off, Jay. You know that singer, Sapphire? Apparently, she hung herself about an hour ago. When I leave here, I gotta head to the scene. The rookie out there doesn't have a clue."

Jay stands in stunned silence and watches Reyes walk off. Tears have been flowing from his face all day, and this just adds to it. Jay walks over to his car and gets in on the passenger side as Shel drives off. He tries to wipe his face.

***

Reyes continues to thumb through the information that Roger left for him. There are all types of notes and some pictures. He smiles with excitement at the information Roger left him. Before he can fully enjoy it, his phone begins to go off. As he reaches to check it, he hears someone else's phone go off, then another, and another. In a matter of seconds, every officer at the funeral seems to be getting a text at the same time. Miesha, Maya, Train, and everyone else looks around confused, as hundreds of phones begin chirping simultaneously.

All of the officers begin looking at their phones. Reyes opens the text message to see Maya's face up close. It was clearly taken at the scene where Roger was killed, as the inside of the warehouse is in the background. It looks like the laptop was set to take a picture when the thumb drive was removed from it. Everyone zeroes in on Maya and pulls their guns. With over five hundred cops standing with their weapons drawn, she knows she doesn't have a chance. Maya gets down on her knees and puts her hands on her head.

"Well-played, Roger Merrit. You win after all," she whispers, nodding with light admiration.

***

Jay and Shel are already zooming down the highway on their way home.

"Are you okay?" asks Shel.

"Not really," Jay responds, looking out the car window.

He takes out his phone and quickly hits the transfer button, sending the last four million to The Ghost's offshore account. Even though he funded Sapphire's demise, the tears are nowhere near stopping. It's just like Roger once told him, *"When you're a hero, eventually a situation will come along that makes you become the villain."*

Made in the USA
Lexington, KY
27 September 2018